'. . . a stunning piece of work, archetypal and human at the same time . . . beautifully written . . . strongly characterised and frighteningly well researched.'

Herbie Brennan

'I loved it and was intrigued from the beautifully written opening paragraphs to the fast-moving conclusion. There's drama all the way through; surprise and excitement as the story unfolds. I love the mix of legends with a new story and the fact that Prague becomes almost a character in the story'

Wendy Cooling

PUPPET MASTER

JOANNE OWEN

PUPPET MASTER

Orion
Children's Books

First published in Great Britain in 2008
by Orion Children's Books
This paperback edition published 2009
by Orion Children's Books
a division of the Orion Publishing Group Ltd
Orion House
5 Upper Saint Martin's Lane
London WC2H 9EA
An Hachette UK Company

1 3 5 7 9 10 8 6 4 2

A catalogue record for this book is available
from the British Library
Printed and bound by Mackays of Chatham, Chatham, Kent

ISBN 978 1 84255 620 7

www.orionbooks.co.uk

Acknowledgements

To my agent, Catherine Clarke, and Wendy Cooling,
for introducing us.
To Renata Clarkova of the London Czech Centre,
for Czech language lessons.
To Becky Stradwick, John Packard and Kate Manning.
To my family, especially my parents, John and Joan, sister
and brother, Katie and James, Auntie and Uncle, Jayne and
Paul, and my grandparents.
To Jesse, Jack, Lily and Mollie.
To everyone at Orion Children's Books,
especially my editor, Fiona Kennedy.

To Lloyd James.

Contents

The Players

Milena Prochazkova
Czech *Milena*, favoured one. The family name, *Prochazka*, derives from the Czech verb to walk.

BoÏena Prochazkova/Baba – Milena's grandmother.
Czech *Božena*, divine gift.

The Master of Marionettes

Zdenko – Protégée of the Master, son of Madam Pinwoman.
Czech *Zdenko*, a winding sheet.

Zdenka – Protégée of the Master, daughter of Madam Pinwoman.
Czech *Zdenka*, a winding sheet.

Lukas Laskavy – Milena's best friend.
Czech *Lukáš*, Luke, meaning "from Lucania"; *Laskav*, warm-hearted, friendly.

Katerina – Milena's aunt, a Doctor of Medicine.
Czech *Katerina*, pure.

Tereza – Milena's aunt, a herbalist
Czech *Tereza*, harvester.

Karel Kopecky – Head Marionette Maker
Czech *Karel*, a free person; *kopeck* one who originates from the hills.

Ludmila Prochazkova/ Maminka – Milena's mother
Czech *Ludmila*, people's favour
Czech *Maminka*, affectionate form of the word for mother.

'Puppets are power, legends are the future.'

Wednesday 12th January, 1898

Beneath the Golden Clock

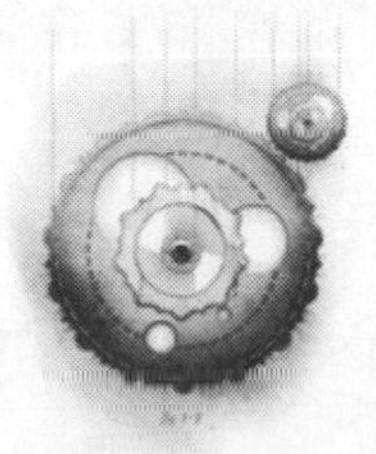

Standing alone on Prague's Old Town Square, a small dark-haired girl with eyes like emeralds and five freckles sprinkled on her nose dances from one foot to the other to keep warm. There's a frozen drinking fountain to her left, an overturned cart to her right and a jumble of buildings all around her. Beneath her feet the icy cobblestones shine and overhead the sky gleams black and silver like coal.

On the eastern edge of the Square the Church of Our Lady Before Tyn dwarfs the buildings around it and is capped by two spires which point to the heavens like a pair of gigantic witches' hats. On the western side stands the white Church of St. Nicholas.

The girl pushes her hands deep into the pockets of her red coat and looks up at the city's famed Astronomical Clock, hoping her friend will arrive before it strikes five. The clock's façade is a series of

black and gold rings which show the days and the months, the rising and setting of the sun, and the waxing and waning, equinoxes and phases of the moon. It shows the course of the planets, the signs of the zodiac as well as the hours, minutes and seconds that mark the passing of each day. Carved animals and plants adorn the edges.

It is almost five o'clock.

Dong

A door bursts open at the top right hand side of the clock. The girl gasps.

Dong

Dong

A wooden statuette of Christ bolts out of the door. She clenches her cold fingers.

Dong

Twelve more figures representing the Apostles emerge in quick succession from the same door. A cockerel leaps from a window at the top of the clock. It crows.

Death emerges from a doorway in the bottom half of the clock, silver bell in one hand, sand-glass in the other. The girl shrinks back, terrified by the sight of Death jerking across the clock face, skeletal jaws agape. He is followed closely by The Turk shaking his head to show he is not yet ready to depart this world. And then comes The Miser clinking a money-bag and The Profligate, gazing into a mirror.

Dong

On the final stroke the figures move back inside the clock.

Milena shivered as a wind from the east whipped around the corner of the Old Town Hall. It felt as if the cold was cutting into her bones. She turned up her collar, eyes still fixed on the clock face. No matter how many times she saw this display, her terror never lessened. Every time Death emerged – shaking his bell, baring his teeth – the story of the master craftsman who had built the clock some four hundred years earlier replayed itself before her eyes.

The tale of how he had been blinded by the city authorities was one of Prague's best-loved and most gruesome legends, and regularly clawed its way into Milena's dreams. As she gazed up at the clock, she could see intruders breaking into his chamber. She saw him being grabbed from behind, being stabbed in both eyes with a hot poker. She heard his flesh fizz, watched him stumble then fall, howling in agony. She felt his heart tumble as he realised he would neither see, nor build another clock.

Milena blew on her fingers and looked across the Square. "Where are you, Lukas?" she said out loud. "Come *on*!" She'd been waiting over twenty minutes for him to arrive.

"And where are you, Maminka?" she whispered. "Are you alone on your birthday? When are you coming home?" No answer came, and no one who knew the Prochazka family believed Milena's mother would ever come home. She'd disappeared three years before, soon after Milena's father, Petr, had died in an accident.

Milena yawned, rubbed her eyes. She'd slept badly, disturbed by another dream of her mother's homecoming. Long before sunrise, she was awake and had run outside, expecting to see her. "One day," she thought, "you *will* come."

Milena spoke to her mother every morning, last thing at night, and very often throughout the day, certain she could hear her, certain that one day she would walk through the door and everything would be as if she had never left. Her father's death had been easier to accept in a way. She had seen his coffin lowered into the ground. She had heard the thud of earth shovelled onto the wood. She knew her father was never going to come back, but she refused to believe she would never see her mother again, and she refused to be called an orphan.

"Where *is* he?" Milena glanced at the clock again. It was twenty minutes past five. She left the Square and went down Zelezna Street, towards the building that used to house her father's marionette theatre. She missed coming here after school. It had been like a second home.

Milena loved everything about the theatre. The thrill

of waiting in the wings before the curtains swished open, the smell of greasepaint in the dressing room, the feel of the plush velvet chairs in the auditorium, the satisfaction she felt as the stories unfolded. And she especially loved marionettes. Watching a puppeteer animate a character with a careful flick of the wrist and a tug on the strings was like witnessing magic. Milena loved the wobbling and nodding of their heads, the satisfying clop of their wooden feet on the stage. And she loved to hear her grandmother's stories about Petr's passion for puppetry. Even before he was able to tie his shoelaces, Baba had told her, he had learned to carve and construct simple marionettes. By the time he was nineteen he had saved enough money to buy this building in Stare Mesto, Prague's Old Town. He transformed it into a theatre named the House of Dream Delights.

Today the windows were boarded up. The once immaculately painted green façade was beginning to crumble. Gone were the bright window boxes of hyacinths and chrysanthemums. Gone was the box office decked out like a stick of striped candy. Milena looked up at the silver sign hanging over the entrance. It was so entangled in twists of ivy she could barely read her father's name.

This was where Milena had taken her first steps and fallen in love with marionettes. And this was where her father had plunged to his death. He'd been positioning a marionette on a platform high above the stage when it had collapsed, sending him headlong onto the boards. As Milena sat on the stone doorstep, clutching her knees to her chest, a lump rose in her throat. It broke her heart to see the theatre like this.

"I'll reopen your House of Dream Delights," she promised. "I'll work and I'll work until I have enough money. That's all that matters. Maminka will come home, and we'll give your theatre new life." She turned to touch the door. A poster had been nailed there. Its edges had been torn by the wind but the message seemed to leap from the cream paper. She wanted to tear it to pieces.

How dare anyone do this to Father's theatre? He was the only real Puppet Master.

But, as she thought of the respect her father had always shown fellow puppeteers, Milena decided he probably wouldn't mind the poster being there.

MARIONETTES
AND HIS
INCREDIBL
TRAVELLING
THEATRE
BOHEMIA
ADMISSION
2
PRESENTS
LEGENDS OF THE FUTUR

The show did look intriguing. She traced a finger around the swirling letters.

The sound of footsteps approaching disturbed her thoughts. "Lukas?" She whirled around. There was no one there. The street was strangely empty.

It came again. The sharp click, click of new boots on stone.

She glanced to the left. Then to the right. Still nothing.

The sound came closer. Milena knew it couldn't be Lukas; his boots were worn thin. Should she slip into the shadows until they had passed? Crouch in the doorway and make herself as small as possible?

As it turned out, there was no time for either.

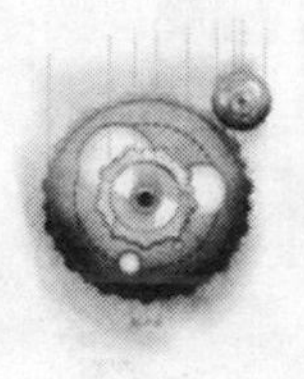

Stare of the Stranger

The footsteps clicked closer and closer.

And then they stopped

"Will you," boomed a voice, "be attending my most marvellous show?"

Milena turned to face the voice and gasped. Shining through the darkness was a pair of glistening yellow eyes. Their calm reptilian blinking horrified her but she found she couldn't look away. The pupils widened, leaving only a dash of colour, like tiny specks of amber in onyx.

Momentarily, the eyes blinked shut, and only then did Milena notice the person they belonged to. An imposing giant whose scarred hands were adorned with gold rings, each so thick they forced his fingers apart. He wore black trousers with gold and red braiding, a black waistcoat, also trimmed with red and gold, and an overcoat with a fox fur collar. Milena was certain; this

was the Master of Marionettes.

"I . . . I don't think so. I'd like to but we don't have the money."

"No money! No money! One of the poor folk, are you?" he snarled. "But," he continued, looking Milena up and down, "if your general deportment and physique – the arch of your brow, the length of your neck – is anything to go by, I believe that at some point, perhaps many moons ago, but certainly at some point, your family may have had some importance . . . But I digress . . ." He lowered his head, locked his eyes on Milena's.

"In my experience, and my experience is considerable – it is as vast as the heavens, as deep as the oceans, as rich as all Bohemia – in my experience, poor folk are little more than animals and, try as they might, there is no way they could fully appreciate the subtle nuances of my show."

Milena restrained herself from wiping the Master's spit from her face. She fidgeted, pulled her coat tight and tried to look away. But again, she couldn't. His eyes held her still. Her head rolled back, her arms dropped to her sides. She no longer felt the cold and she was no longer aware of where she was.

"So, you've nothing to say?" scoffed the Master, pacing around Milena like a fox circling a chicken pen. "Where's your gumption? Your mettle? Your pluck, your sense of pride? Your family must be ashamed to have brought such a meek and miserable creature into this world. Am I right, hmm? Am I not right?" he demanded.

"But you can't hear a word I'm saying, can you?"

"You're wrong," replied Milena. She *could* hear him. She had managed to hurl herself back into the real world. She was aware of the wind and the frost and the grizzly bear of a man standing over her.

"You're wrong," she repeated, staring into his eyes, as resolutely as his had invaded hers. "You know nothing about me, nothing at all, so keep your thoughts to yourself!" She lowered her gaze. "If you don't mind," she added quietly.

The Puppet Master's face turned beetroot red; his chest expanded, the veins on his forehead bulged. His whole body trembled. Just as it looked as if he might explode with rage, he let out an almighty roar of laughter. Milena thought the whole city would feel its reverberations, from the top of the castle high on the hill, to the muddy depths of the river bed. The laugh went on and on. Eventually it subsided and he began to speak.

"Remarkable," he laughed. "All my life I have played with people the way a cat might tease a mouse. I circle them, psychologically speaking, sometimes physically, you understand, creating dread, observing their terror grow and grow until it takes over their being from the inside out. I watch the colour drain from their cheeks, and then I turn with a swish of my coat and leave them, with uncertainty and fear burning right into their very core. I control them. What else would a Puppet Master do, but pull people's strings? But you, you answered back. I applaud you."

"Mi-lena!" Lukas' voice rang out. "Mi-lena, where are you?"

"I am certain we shall meet again. Very soon, in fact." The Master glanced over his shoulder. "Zdenko, Zdenka, to my carriage!"

Two short figures swathed in hooded cloaks emerged from the shadows and stood either side of him. Shiny round-toed shoes jutted out beneath the billowing black cloth.

The Master departed with a swoosh of his coat. The hooded figures followed, so close it looked as if he had extra limbs.

"I guessed you'd be here, but who were *they*?" called Lukas, hurrying towards Milena. "Are you all right?" he asked, laying a hand on her shoulder.

He and Milena had been best friends for longer than Lukas could remember. No-one understood him like she did. They couldn't have been closer. "I'm really sorry I'm late."

"Where were you? I got bored waiting on the Square.

Lukas dismissed Milena's crossness with a wave of his arm. "I'm here now, and just in time by the look of things. What did they want?"

"I'm really not sure ***what*** they wanted," Milena

frowned. "The man is the Puppet Master in charge of this show. He appeared from nowhere, and I suddenly began to feel very odd, as if I was in a dream. But look, it says it's a 'once in a lifetime experience'. It opens on Friday. I'd love to see it."

Lukas read the poster. "So would I, but it's too expensive. Anyway, let's go. I didn't like the look of him. He's made you as jumpy as a jack-in-the-box. Look at you, you're shaking. You know my mother would have had a fit if she'd seen him. She's always been terrified of puppets, ever since she was little. 'Dancing corpses', that's what she calls them."

"She shouldn't be afraid of them, they're not exactly dead. It's more as though they're always between life and death, waiting to become whatever the puppeteer needs them to be. That's what Father used to say."

"I don't think that would make her feel any better," Lukas laughed. "Here, take my gloves before your fingers turn to icicles."

Nestled deep in the valley formed by seven hills, the city was draped in the darkness of a winter evening as Milena and Lukas set off, chatting about what they'd done during the day. Almost every street corner they passed was occupied by a chestnut roaster or pretzel-seller calling to customers. The aroma of chestnuts blistering on hot coals filled their noses. All across the city squares emptied as market stalls were cleared of goods and packed away for the night. Rattling trams filled with bleary eyed office clerks who had put their papers to one side, and with factory machinists who had shut down their clanking machines. Inside, wives and mothers put pots on to boil, stoked fires and called their children off the streets and out of parks.

As they stepped in front of him, a toymaker took a wooden bird from a cloth laid at his feet. He wound it and placed it on his grubby hand.

"Good evening!" he called, nodding to Milena and Lukas in turn. "Can you spare a moment to view my wares? Observe how he flaps his wings and pecks my palm! Sir, I think your friend would love to take this fine fellow home with her. I have plenty more, look! Every colour, every size, every type of bird you could wish for."

The toymaker lunged towards the ground with the unpredictability of a madman. His eyes darted from one to the next as he wound up all the birds and set them hopping and pecking and whirring across the cloth.

"Look at them go! Cheep, cheep little birds! Would you like me to name one after you? What are you called?"

"Milena Prochazkova," Milena answered politely.

"How about this one, Milena? I'll give you a good price. Or how about this furry fellow?" He pulled a clockwork mouse from his pocket, turned the key on its back, set it scuttling about the ground. "I only need a coin or two to buy a sausage for my supper."

"They're all very nice, but I'm afraid we can't afford one," said Milena.

The toymaker kicked out at the birds. "They're all very nice, but I'm afraid we can't afford one," he mocked in a squeaky voice. "Don't lie to me. You can't be short of a crown or two."

"I'm not lying," Milena insisted. "We really can't."

"Think you're better than me, do you?" he hissed, tossing the jittering toys into a sack. "Think you're too good for my birds? You'll be sorry when my birds have gone."

Milena pulled a coin from her pocket. "Take this," she offered. "It's not enough for a bird, but it's all I have."

"Really?" asked the toymaker. "That's really all you have?"

Milena nodded.

"Thank you for your kindness." He took the coin, threw the bundle of birds over his back and disappeared down a side street.

"I hope he'll be all right," said Milena as he vanished from view.

"Don't worry about him. You tried to help. Come on, Baba will be wondering where you are."

But Milena was worried about the toymaker. She suspected the birds were his only companions. She wished she'd had enough to buy one. Baba had taught her to be generous, and she'd never forgotten her tale of the Conceited Tradeswoman. She could hear it now, as clearly as if Baba were whispering in her ear.

The Tale of the Conceited Tradeswoman

The Conceited Tradeswoman was a shrewd creature who made a living buying poultry from country people and selling them in Prague for great profit. One day a farmer came from Jilove and sold her a dozen chickens for a very good price. She felt like having chicken for her dinner so she cut one open and, to her delight, discovered several grains of gold in its stomach. Greedy as she was, the tradeswoman cut open the rest of the chickens and there, inside each of the plump creatures was grain after grain after grain of glittering gold. She couldn't believe her good fortune.

When the farmer returned a week later he agreed to sell her more of his hens if she promised never to sell them on to anyone else. She agreed and soon became one of the richest people in Prague, but she never shared her wealth with anyone.

A few weeks later the Tradeswoman was on her way to collect rent from one of her tenants when an elderly beggar stopped her as she crossed Karluv Bridge.

"Good lady, could you spare me a crown?" the old woman called. "My husband is dead, my children have left me, I'm all alone in this cruel world. Please lady, I haven't eaten for days."

The Tradeswoman tossed her hair and looked away in disgust.

"May you have to beg yourself one day!" the old woman shouted after her. "May you know what it is to be poor and hungry."

The Tradeswoman turned back and pulled a gold ring from her finger. She threw it into the Vltava saying, "As I shall never see this ring again, so your words will never come true!"

That same evening she hosted a feast in one of her mansions. As her guests tucked in to their meals, she cut the fish on her own plate and, to her horror, there inside was the gold ring she had thrown over the bridge. The colour drained from her face as she remembered the words of the beggar woman.

The very next day the Tradeswoman learned that she'd been cheated out of a business deal, that one of her houses had been burgled, that another had burned down. Within a week she was destitute, left with nothing but the clothes on her back and the gold ring that had returned to her in the fish. This time she did not haughtily toss the ring into the river; she sold it to a goldsmith so she could buy some food and then went to Karluv Bridge to find the beggar woman. But she wasn't there so the Tradeswoman sat on the stones, lowered her head and held out her hand, hoping someone would find it in their heart to help her. Many people passed her by, but none offered her so much as a crust of bread. Then, as the sun set, she felt someone press a coin into her palm. She opened her eyes and saw the old beggar woman, dressed as finely as a nobleman's wife.

And the lesson to be learned is that she who helps others will be helped. Fortunes rise and fortunes fall, faster than a ferret down a rabbit hole.

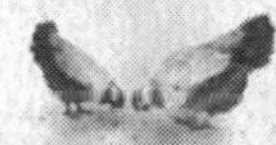

Hurrying through the damp arcades and narrow, cobbled alleys of the Old Town, Milena felt the toymaker's loneliness in every person they passed. She saw it in the hunched shoulder of the vagrants who crouched between the crooked headstones of the Jewish Cemetery in Josefov. She saw it in the trembling hands of the old woman who sat in the doorway of the Church of St. Michael's Mystery, pleading with passersby to buy pieces of her lace. And she glimpsed it in the eyes of the beggar boy on the corner of Jilska and Karlova.

As they walked across Karluv Bridge, which spanned the Vltava River linking the eastern and western districts of Prague, it felt to Milena as if the waters were shooting tiny splinters of ice at her cheeks, as if the stone statues of saints which flanked either side of the bridge were about to gather her up in their cold grey arms. She could see the bloody fingers of the stonemason who had given his soul to the Devil in exchange for his help rebuilding the bridge gripping the outer wall. A lone swan beneath the bridge opened its wings and soared away, strong and graceful as it journeyed in search of its partner.

Milena took hold of Lukas' arm and they tramped, silently now, through the Lesser Quarter, climbed Nerudova Hill and finally reached the Castle District which sparkled beneath the white light of a full moon.

At the House of the Golden Acorn

Baba smiled as she closed the oven door on the roasting rabbit. "Milena will enjoy this!" Her back ached from bending over a washing tub in their yard for hours in the cold. But Baba was not one to complain. She had to make sure everything was as perfect as possible for Milena's return. She moved nimbly around the kitchen as she put the used dishes and dirty spoons into the sink.

Baba's kitchen was the heart of the cottage, where she and Milena spent most of their time together. It had a curved stone ceiling, and nooks and crannies crammed with tins of flour, pots of dried herbs, jars of paprika and caraway seeds. A pitcher of milk stood just inside the door, chilled by the icy draughts that shot through the cottage. A string of hairy onions hung from a hook above the stove and a jar of boiled cinnamon and vanilla

sweets was tucked into a gap between the windowsill and sink.

Baba took pride in everything she did. Every day she dressed *properly*. She polished her boots until they shone. Her skirts were threadbare but they were always immaculately clean and pressed, and she never left the house without pinning up her silver hair and putting on her fur-edged leather gloves and hat.

But while Baba outwardly appeared full of good cheer, inside she grappled with grief; she hadn't forgiven herself for failing to keep her son's theatre open. She had been forced to sell both the House of Dream Delights and their home near the riverbank. But at least she had laid Petr to rest in the National Cemetery at Vysehrad, where all the great Czech artists, writers and musicians were buried.

Baba kept her troubles hidden from Milena. She knew Milena relived her father's accident daily, saw him swoop towards the stage like a bird whose wings failed to support his flight. And she knew Milena heard her mother calling to her every night. "She's coming. She's coming home!" she would cry in her sleep and Baba would rush to calm her.

Even during the daytime Milena was often convinced she had felt her mother's presence; through a rain storm that sprung unexpectedly from a summer sky, a breeze that brought a leaf to rest at her feet. Baba had come to realise that she had been wrong to keep things from her granddaughter. "I should have known you can't put your troubles in a bottle and send them all away," she thought. "The sea will simply wash it back. Perhaps the time has come for me to unseal the bottle and tell Milena everything."

She read through the recipe she had written in her brown leather notebook several decades ago, added a pinch more parsley and dipped her little finger into the sauce that simmered on the stove.

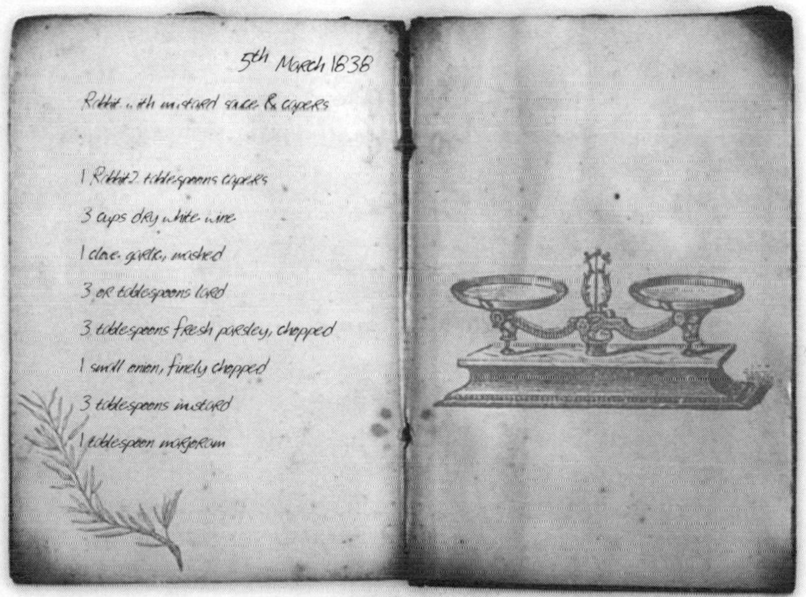

5th March 1838

Rabbit with mustard sauce & capers

1 Rabbit 2 tablespoons capers
3 cups dry white wine
1 clove garlic, mashed
3 or tablespoons lard
3 tablespoons fresh parsley, chopped
1 small onion, finely chopped
3 tablespoons mustard
1 tablespoon marjoram

A dog barked outside, and Baba peeped through the curtains. Although this part of the city had long been home to the city's nobility, the smaller streets located down the winding hill to the east of Castle Square were occupied largely by the castle's servants. It was on one of these that Baba and Milena lived, on a street called Novy Svet, in a cottage called the House of the Golden Acorn.

Novy Svet was a welcoming place. Each cottage was painted a different colour – sky blue, mint green, rose-pink, lemon or lilac. In spring and summer the scent of roses and honeysuckle drifted along the lane, and in winter the smell of log fires and paprika-spiced goulash puffed out of chimneys and escaped through kitchen windows.

She loved to feel thousands of years of Prague's history all around her in the Castle District. It was as if the souls of folk from bygone days lingered in every stone of every palace, seeped from every spire of every church. Whenever she strolled at night she heard the haunting melodies of long-dead court musicians glide over the rooftops of the Old Burgravary and across Stag Moat, or the frustrated cries of Emperor Rudolf's alchemists echo down Golden Lane.

"I've become very fond of the Castle District," Baba would say to her sisters-in-law, Katerina and Tereza, whenever they suggested she and Milena should move in with them. "I could happily spend the rest of my days here." And besides, Baba believed that "the pocket must be filled by she who wears the apron". She was too proud to accept charity from anyone.

Baba opened the stove door to check on the roasting meat. A rich rabbity smell spilled out. "Delicious! Now where's Milena? It's not like her to be late."

At the House of the Ladies of the Snow

Milena's aunts were sitting in the drawing room of the family home, southeast of Old Town Square, not far from the National Museum.

"Do you remember what day it is today?" asked Tereza quietly.

Katerina looked up from her scientific journal. "Of course I do," she nodded. "It's Ludmila's birthday. Three years to the day since she went. I'm beginning to think we'll never know what happened to her."

"We should be grateful for what time we had with her," replied Tereza. "We were blessed to have had such an extraordinary sister. We were always the Sisters of the Snow and she our Sister of the Sun." She fastened the lid on the jar of henbane she had been examining and made a note in her *Diary of Herbal Experimentation*.

Findings from 12th January, 1898

HENBANE (otherwise known as Hogsbean, Devil's Eye or Black Nightshade)

PHYSICAL DESCRIPTION - grows on waste ground and has hairy, sticky leaves, a sickening smell and bell shaped dark veined yellow flowers.

HISTORY - In Greek legend the dead in Hades were crowned with Henbane as they wandered beside the River Styx.

USES - The plant has been used since antiquity for its power to cause delirium and hallucinations. Wear about your person to attract love. Burn outdoors to bring rain, although this may intensify the plant's toxicity.

NOTE: crushing between your fingers is likely to cause irritation.

WORMWOOD

(otherwise known as Artemsia absintuium, Old Woman, Crown for a King)

PHYSICAL DESCRIPTION - Grows naturally on dry uncultivated ground, such as rocky slopes. Leaves are green-grey above, white below and covered in fine silver hairs. Its flowers are pale yellow.

HISTORY - The word 'wormwood' is derived from Middle English 'wormwode' (at the time the plant was used as a cure for intestinal worms).

USES - Burn in incense to increase psychic powers and summon spirits. The plant's oil can also be used to improve circulation. It is an ingredient in absinthe, a highly intoxicating alcoholic beverage, and can also be used to make wine. Pure wormwood oil is very poisonous but with correct dosage poses little danger.

BELLADONNA

(otherwise known as Banewort, Nightshade, Death's Herb, Naughty Man's Cherries, Witch's Berry)

PHYSICAL DESCRIPTION - has a white, thick, fleshy root, dull dark green oval leaves and dark purple, bell-shaped flowers. Its berry is cherry-sized and full of an inky, sweet poisonous juice.

HISTORY - worshippers of Bellona, Roman Goddess of war, drank an infusion of belladonna prior to invoking her spirit. Found chiefly in the Carpathian region of Poland, this plant has long been associated with witches and appears in most old flying ointment recipes.

USES - Leaves and root are narcotic, hallucinogenic and sedative. It can be used as an anaesthetic. It is highly toxic, potentially deadly.

Symptoms of poisoning by belladonna include the loss of the voice, frequent bending forward and rocking of the upper body and constant movement of the fingers. The pupils of the eyes become much dilated.

"I think I'll leave my work for today," Tereza sighed, rubbing her blistered hands on her gown.

"If truth be told, I'm not at all in the right frame of mind for reading either. I've been staring at the same sentence for the past ten minutes," said Katerina, removing her wire spectacles and putting the journal to one side.

She stood and walked to the window. Two young figures were hurrying along the street below, laughing and chatting loudly. It was their neighbour's daughter and her fiancé. Katerina tapped on the window and waved to them before drawing the curtains.

"What a charming couple they make. It's strange to think that in no time at all Milena might be courting herself. He will have to be a *very* special young man. Warm of heart, considerate in spirit. I suppose I needn't worry; Milena knows her own mind and would never settle for second best. But I still wish she and Baba would come and live with us. We have more than enough room."

"We should have been together this evening, for Ludmila's birthday, but at least she and Lukas are coming tomorrow. Katerina," said Tereza, glancing coyly at her older sister, "do you think the time may have come for me to see if Milena shares my intuition for herb-working? What do you think? We could begin with something simple. Perhaps a little light weather manipulation. Or I could show her how to concoct a few easy remedies. After all, Ludmila did entrust all three of us with her education."

"I don't doubt that Milena has inherited your talents, but we must be patient," Katerina warned, raising her eyebrows. "Baba thinks she's far too over-excitable as it is."

"Perhaps you're right, but we shouldn't leave it too long. Anyway, we should do something to honour Ludmila's birthday. Let's go to the garden and say a few words for her."

As Tereza stood and rearranged her skirts she noticed a green stain spreading across the rug. She gasped. "I'm sorry. I've ruined the rug with Virginia dogwood."

"That, Tereza, was hand-woven by a Hungarian master-weaver over one hundred years ago. It's irreplaceable. You really should restrict yourself to working in the cellar. And perhaps you might like to read some of my medical journals. We're no longer in the days of the wise-women, you know. But I suppose a blemish on a rug doesn't matter in the grand scheme of things."

They walked to the kitchen their dresses rustling like the first leaf fall of autumn. Even though they had spent the day at home, and had received no visitors, they were dressed as if they were going out for dinner, or to the opera. Katerina wore a high-necked, floor length black taffeta dress. She had scraped her hair into a tight coil which pulled her eyes into a severe stare and her cheekbones to two sharp points. Tereza's face was powdered bone white, except for the rouge on her cheeks, and she wore a similarly styled purple dress and an emerald brooch.

Had their house not been so grand it might have seemed odd to dress so formally, but against the backdrop of embroidered silk drapes and huge framed oil paintings, they looked entirely appropriate. It could be said the house was too large for two people but being the eldest, Katerina had inherited the family home. While they had once been affluent, employing a cook and maid, now their only remaining employee was their carriage driver, Mr. Kolar.

Tereza opened the back door and they went outside. Their garden was thick with the fir trees the three sisters had planted when they were young, and to the right of the kitchen door Tereza had cleared space for a herb garden so she could grow everything she needed for her remedies. Burdock, nutmeg, fennel, rosemary, sage and peppermint and all kinds of pungent-smelling plants grew within a rectangular patch.

Tereza picked a burdock leaf from her patch of plants. She held the leaf above the candle flame until fine wisps of smoke rushed from its edges.

"Wherever you might be, our hearts are with you." She blew into the smoke and it carried her kiss away. "May the goodness of this leaf find its way to you and keep you from harm."

A single snowflake landed on her nose. She smiled. "Happy Birthday, Ludmila."

The Convoy

A procession of painted wagons trundled through Prague's Old Town. Their red and gold wheels turned slowly, for the loads they bore were weighty. Their shutters and doors were firmly sealed so no one could glimpse the secrets they carried. Drawn by two dozen horses whose hooves clattered over the cobblestones of the Square, the procession halted abruptly near the Astronomical Clock. As the masked drivers pulled the reins taut, the horses hauling the wagon at the head of the procession snorted and flared their nostrils. Their feathered headdresses, one cobalt blue, the other cherry red, quivered.

Three figures emerged from the darkness. The first tall and heavily built, the two who followed short and slight. They climbed into the lead wagon and the

convoy resumed its journey towards Karluv Bridge.

The clouds shifted and moonlight struck a doll left lying stiff on the doorstep of the Old Town Hall.

The Legacy of Libuse

Baba hurried to the cottage door as she heard a key turn in the latch.

"Come in, come in! Supper is ready. We have parsnips, potatoes, fried cheese and a delicious rabbit courtesy of Mr. Hajek. He went out to the forest this morning and caught one especially for us. You know how he hates anyone to shop for what can be caught in the country.

"Take off your coat and boots. Would you mind cutting the bread while I carve the rabbit? But take care that it's cut straight, Milenka, for whoever doesn't cut

their bread evenly will never come out even with people."

Milena threw her arms around her Grandmother's waist. She still loved it when Baba called her Milenka, little Milena. It was the name her parents had always called her.

She picked up a knife and cut the bread carefully and very, very evenly. They sat down to eat.

"This is delicious," said Milena as she sunk her teeth into the soft meat. Being with Baba for a few minutes had already made her feel much better. All thoughts of the toymaker and Puppet Master had, for the time being at least, left her mind.

"I'm very glad you're home. I was beginning to worry," said Baba, cutting into a piece of creamy fried cheese. "You haven't forgotten that you and Lukas are visiting your aunts for tea tomorrow, have you? Mr. Kolar will collect you from school. I hope they've stocked up their larder. You two have stomachs like goats!"

Milena smiled. Baba was the same every evening; full of cheer, always eager to please. "Of course I haven't forgotten. I love visiting them. They make me feel like a princess."

"And you *are* a princess. Now tell me what you did at school today."

Milena pulled a sheet of paper from her pocket. "I wrote this."

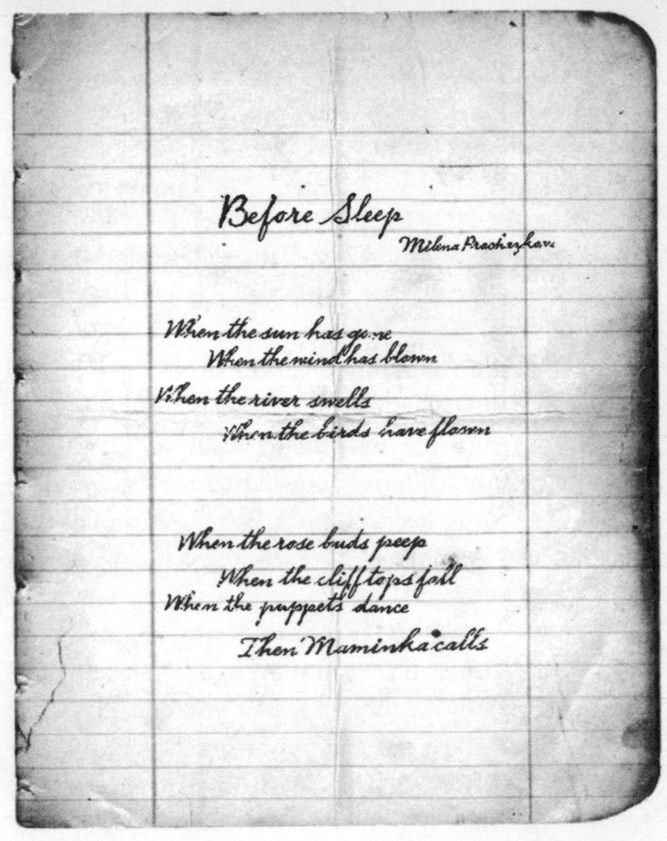

Before Sleep

Milena Prochazkova

When the sun has gone
When the wind has blown
When the river swells
When the birds have flown

When the rose buds peep
When the cliff tops fall
When the puppets dance
Then Maminka calls

"Miss Slovakova asked me to read it out, which means she can't have thought it was too bad. She would never say so, though, in case the praise goes to our heads. Tomorrow we're going to learn about the legends and myths of Old Bohemia."

Baba's eyes flashed. "Good for you, Milena, good for you. You're as sharp as a hare is sprightly, just like your mother. She loved to write stories and poems."

"Weren't you going to say anything about it being her birthday?"

"I'm sorry, I thought it might upset you." Baba had finished eating and, moving from the table to sit down in her rocking chair, reached out, and took hold of Milena's hands. "I know you miss her, we all do. But you must take heart in the fact that you meant the world to your mother and father. They would have given you the very blue from the sky, the glorious green from the grass. Let's leave the dishes. Come and sit by the fire. I have something to tell you about Maminka. Something we shouldn't have kept from you for so long."

"What do you mean? Do you know why she went? Are you sure we tried hard enough to find her?"

"We did all we could. The city authorities, our friends and neighbours spent the night scouring the Old Town and the Lesser Quarter, asking at inns, checking churches and parks, and when the sun rose we started to search the city, and then the outlying villages.

"Aunt Tereza was convinced that she was so distressed by your father's death that she'd fled to Divoka Sarka Forest. She loved to walk there so we searched, just in case. Then a few nights later your classmate Ruzena and her brother went missing too. Those were strange days."

"Don't worry," Milena interrupted. "We'll see her again. I dreamed she came home again last night. That's the third time this week. She was at the top of the lane, waiting for me. When I went outside she wasn't there, but she'll come. I know she will."

Baba shook her head. "No, Milena, she won't. You must accept that she's gone. Your father and mother will live in your heart forever, but," Baba continued, lowering her voice, "neither are ever coming back. All this waiting and hoping is crippling your soul, making you weak, yet you need to be the strongest girl in all Bohemia. Your destiny demands great things of you, and the time has come for you to understand why.

"Let me start at the beginning and proceed with care, for you should never rush baking a decent bun, no matter how hungry you might be. I'm going to tell you the story of Maminka's family, a story which takes us back to the very beginnings of Bohemia, to a time when legends were made."

Baba leaned over the side of her rocking chair and poked the fire, casting leaping shadows across the ceiling. The room seemed as hot and small as an oven and Milena felt as if she was being roasted. Her skin prickled and strands of hair stuck to her forehead. She edged back from the hearth and noticed that her grandmother looked very old and very tired. Perhaps it was the light, but the flesh beneath her eyes looked thinner than gossamer, as if the slightest touch might tear it, and the skin on her trembling hands was almost transparent.

"This," said Baba, "is the tale of your life. Settle yourself and listen."

Chapter One

Libuse and Her Sister

"Many thousands of years ago there were three wise and fearless brothers – Cech, Lech and Rus – who spent their days and nights leading their people. No forest was too thick, no animal too fierce to hinder their expedition. After some months had passed they reached a high point of land. When the dawn mist cleared they saw wonderful forests, alive with bristly wild boar and deer. Three great rivers, the Ohre, the Elbe and the Vltava, stretched below them, running swift as slender eels.

"As the brothers gazed upon this spectacular sight, overlooking the place where the three rivers met, they decided to go their separate ways and each follow the flow of a different river. Rus and his family and followers went east, while Lech and his family and followers headed west, and Cech led his people south.

"After travelling for almost a year Cech's people began to feel weary of forever wandering and never settling, so they gathered together and asked him to find a permanent place to make their home. Being a good man, Cech listened to what his people wanted. He left the camp and climbed the mountain Rip to enjoy a better view of their location. When he reached its peak his eyes were drawn to an area of dense woodland and dark meadows. It was sliced in two by a silver river. He shouted down from the mountain to his people, 'Here we shall stay.'

"And there they stayed. Soon a village was born and everyone was content with the land they occupied and the life that good Brother Cech enabled them to lead. But after a few years he died, and the people needed a new leader. Everyone agreed that the best person for the job was Krok, Cech's eldest son, for he was very much like his father – strong and kind and just. He was hailed the new head of the tribe and from that day on was known as King Krok.

"They built him a new castle called Budec near the village of Zbecno. In time Krok and his wife were blessed with three remarkable daughters. Their firstborn, Kasa, was a sharp-witted girl who grew up to be highly skilled in medicine. She could change a man's fate, and people believed so strongly in her powers that they said of things that were hopelessly lost 'even Kasa could not bring that back.' In time she left Budec Castle and established a clan around her own castle, Kasin.

"Their second-born, Teta, understood the ways of nature and grew up to be a priestess and spiritual guardian of the people. She instructed that a statue of her goddess, Klimba, be built on a mountaintop to watch over and protect the tribe.

"And then came Krok's youngest daughter, Libuse, the wisest and most beautiful of them all. She studied at the first school in Bohemia and learned all there was to know about the healing properties of herbs, such as the protective powers of sewing woodruff into a leather pouch, or how wearing coriander seeds can ease an aching head. She learned which plants do good and which do harm, and she learned how to track deer in the forest, how to escape bear attacks, and how to make the finest kind of hunting spear.

"But most incredible of all, she experienced visions which showed her what the future would bring. She knew when her father and his men would enjoy a successful hunt, and she knew when it would be fruitless to venture into the depths of the forests. She knew when farmers should safeguard their crops from ravaging storms and she knew what would come to pass in the future.

"Every day Libuse mounted her white horse and rode around the grounds of King Krok's castle or galloped through the surrounding forests. She stayed with her parents until she had learned everything the school could teach her and then left the family castle to build her own. Stronger than her sisters' strongholds, stronger even than Budec, she named it Libusin.

"After his three daughters had left, and by now nearing the end of his life, King Krok built a castle on a high, rocky place above the Vltava River so his people would be safe for centuries to come, long after he had passed away. It was named Vysehrad, the High Castle, and was famed for its impenetrability."

"The Vltava! That's our river!" said Milena, glad that at least some of Baba's story was beginning to sound familiar. "And Vysehrad is where Father is buried. But I don't remember seeing a castle, just the church and gardens."

"Yes, there's not much of the original castle left now, only ruins of the old watch tower, but for centuries it was the most impressive building in the land."

"Sadly, soon after settling into his new castle, Krok's long and noble life came to an end, and the people were without a leader. The elders of the tribe met to decide what to do. And it became clear that, even though she was a young woman, Libuse's wisdom and graciousness and prophetic visions made her the obvious successor to the throne. Honoured that the elders considered her suitable to assume her father's role, Libuse moved to Vysehrad and took up her duties immediately."

Milena crossed and uncrossed her legs, stretched her arms. "Thank you Baba, but why is it *my* story? What does it have to do with *me*?"

"It has everything to do with you. You, through your mother's family line, are a descendent of the great Queen Libuse. If you were to follow the path of history back in time it would lead you directly to her. Your Maminka carried the Legacy of Libuse, and I'm certain that you do too."

Milena felt a frisson of excitement. Her breathing quickened.

"Milena? Milena, what is it?"

"Nothing's wrong," she smiled, her eyes radiant. "I've always known there was something special about Maminka. But what exactly is the Legacy of Libuse? What does it mean to carry it?"

"Just as Libuse foresaw what would come to pass, so did your mother. That is the legacy. Usually her visions were heralded by a sharp pain in the temples, light-headedness. At other times she found herself in the middle of one without warning.

"Sometimes she foresaw good things. She knew, for example, that she would meet the love of her life at the opening of the House of Dream Delights. But she foresaw tragedy too; the burning of the National Theatre, the flooding of the Vltava eight years ago. Even though she managed to convince the authorities to fire cannons from Vysehrad to alert people, the vision and warning came too late. The swelling waters were so powerful that part of Karluv Bridge had collapsed even before the last cannon fired.

"Your mother never forgave herself for not

responding to the vision more quickly. Libuse's legacy became a burden, so she strove to suppress it. I can't imagine how difficult it must have been for her, knowing people would suffer or even die, but being unable to prevent it from happening."

"Why didn't she tell me any of this?" Milena asked. "And if she could see into the future, wouldn't she have known that Father was going to die, or that she would be separated from us?"

"She wanted to protect you. Perhaps she hoped the legacy would pass you by if she managed to ignore her own visions. But I'm certain she knew your father was in danger. Remember how she turned white as freshly fallen snow and ran from the house calling to your father. But by the time she'd reached the theatre he had already left this world. And before the hour had passed, she had gone missing.

"As time goes on and you grow older, I feel more certain that you, Milena, like Ludmila, carry the Legacy of Libuse. Just as she knew your father was in danger, you had been curiously anxious to go to the theatre to see your father all day. And your dreams and nightmares could be signs of the legacy too. We'll have to wait and see."

"We don't need to wait. I already know. That's what she's been trying to tell me."

"You should rest," said Baba. "Your aunts will be delighted to tell you more tomorrow. They've been waiting for this day for years." She coaxed Milena to her feet.

"Try to sleep. When the morning comes, you'll see the world through new eyes."

In Wood She Rests, as Wood Shall She Rise

The Puppet Master was feeling pleased with himself. He loved few things more than putting on a new show, and here they were at last, in Prague, about to reveal *The Legends of the Future* to the world. It was cold, but the frost in the air gave the city a certain sharply defined beauty. The absence of rain was welcome, for the ground was solid enough for the troupe to set up securely at their base, not too far from the river, at the foot of Petrin Hill.

He was glad to be back in Prague, and even more glad to see that the city was packed with thousands of people who would come to his show. He rubbed his hands at the thought of how easy it was going to be to realise his ambitions. "Easy prey, the whole lot of them!" he snarled.

A feast was spread on the table before him. Three whole roast ducks stuffed with plums and hazelnuts sat beside a paprika poached carp, garnished with parsley and thick wedges of lemon. Fried potatoes, soaked in sour cream, steamed in a glass bowl and veal tongue stewed in mustard seeds and onions sat on a silver platter. There was so much food, that just looking at it would make a normal person feel queasy. But not the Master. He was not a normal person. He gulped down a goblet of red wine and bit into a boar's meat sausage.

"Delicious!"

A boy materialised from behind a chair and sidled up to the Master. "Have you had enough, sir?" he asked.

"Indeed I have not, Zdenko," he spluttered through the second sausage. Fat dribbled from the corners of his mouth. "Bring me more . . ."

Precisely on cue, as if she were following a script, Zdenko's twin sister emerged and refilled the Master's goblet.

"Wine?" she offered.

"Never one without the other!" laughed the Master. "How perceptive, Zdenka. You're both developing devilishly well. It's impossible to see in your faces what your minds are thinking. What brilliantly dispassionate creatures you are."

The twins looked at one another, twisted their lips into a wry smile. They always knew what the other was thinking. And, while their bodies looked painfully thin and their faces ashen, they possessed the confidence and poise of the worldly-wise. Their formal clothes and austere demeanor made them much seem older than their years. A skinny plait tied with green silk ribbon sprouted from either side of Zdenka's head. Round-toed, silver-buckled shoes poked like shiny beetles from her legs. She straightened her dress, ran a cold finger down the row of green buttons that fastened it.

Zdenko looked like an undertaker's apprentice in his black velvet suit and starched white shirt. His side-parted hair was like the wings of a raven: sleek, black, neat. He twitched his left ear. Zdenka responded with a snigger and flare of her right nostril. They positioned themselves at the end of the table.

"How crafty. I barely saw you move," the Master praised. "Not long now until I unleash your cunning upon the people of Prague. You have a tremendous theatrical career ahead of you."

"Thank you, Master," said Zdenka, hardly moving a muscle on her heart-shaped face, "but I'm not sure we can wait any longer."

"Your enthusiasm is commendable, Zdenka, but, while I'm confident my marionettes are the most life-like cast this undeserving world will ever witness, there remains a tremendous amount of work to be done. This must be the most exquisite show anyone has ever seen. If you serve me well, you'll enjoy far greater status than being assistants to a Puppet Master. This is my home-coming!"

The twins blinked, Zdenka a fraction earlier than her brother, winning her the right to respond first. "I'm not sure we understand exactly what you mean, Master, but we're eager to learn . . . "

". . . everything you can teach us," Zdenko concluded.

"And you will. Simply allow yourselves to absorb the wisdom I impart. Make yourselves receptive to my powers. And obey me. Obey me down to the very last wink, nod or prod. Although," the Master continued, pushing aside his empty plate, "your blood runs with such malevolence that I sometimes think I've done my job too well."

The twins smirked. The Master was right. He had taught them well. But he couldn't claim all the glory for developing their wicked streak. Their mother said they'd been that way inclined since the day they were born.

Zdenko edged towards Zdenka, entwined a finger around her thumb. She tapped her heels on the floor.

"Stop that. Come. I must see how the preparations are progressing. Anyone caught doing anything other than executing my instructions will be put on a diet of horse droppings for a week. Fasten my boots boy, or I'll snip off your fingers! Snip, snip, snip, snip. I'll be generous and leave you a thumb. Come along."

Zdenko knelt before the Master and buckled his tough leather boots. The Master stood, then went to the door. He unlocked the top half and gazed wistfully at Petrin Tower. Its metal framework stood spindly and black atop the peak, a short distance from the end of the funicular railway line which carried visitors up and down the hill along a single steep track every day until dusk.

"My green jewel in the heart of Bohemia's crown," he murmured, watching his workers as they transformed Petrin Hill into a magnificent showground. A procession of children heaved painted wooden scenery boards and caskets of stage props across the grass. His strongest men were assembling a full scale wooden theatre; even though his show was a travelling one the Master saw no reason to compromise on his venue. His show would ***never*** be performed in a mere tent.

"Good evening, Madam Pinwoman," he called to the twins' mother, his Head Seamstress, who he had re-named on account of her looking like a walking pin cushion: plump, and always covered in needles and strands of thread. "I hope the costumes are nearing completion. Don't forget, you'll be disciplined if there's so much as a sequin out of place. And that goes for all of you!" The group of giggling girls she was leading through the camp fell silent.

"They'll be ready, have no fear," promised Madam Pinwoman. "I hope you two are behaving yourselves. Come straight home to me once the Master's finished with you for the night."

"Of course we shall, Mother," the twins replied in a uniformly monotone voice. They raised an arm and waved, mechanical as clockwork toys.

Madam Pinwoman shook her head. "I'm beginning to wonder if they're mine or fashioned by you, Master, as I fashion the clothes your puppets wear. It pains me to say it but, with the passing of each day, I seem to have less and less control over them."

Her eyes met his. He looked away. "They'll be home once I've finished with them. Carry on. You're holding everyone up."

Madam Pinwoman's seamstresses were closely followed by a cart loaded with musicians, their instruments and the choir. As they passed the Master the band leader nudged his fellow musicians and they began to play. "That's it, keep up with the practice!" the Master bellowed. "And what charming voices the young ladies have. If they ever see them again, which is, admittedly, extremely unlikely, but if they do ever see them again, their parents will be very proud of them for having learned so much so quickly. Who would have thought girls from such lowly origins could develop into such sweet songbirds? Take note, Zdenko, Zdenka, that's what I can do for people. I identify their talents, nurture them, shape new lives. If I hadn't snatched them away from their miserable families they'd still be milking cows on their fathers' farms, not preparing to perform in front of thousands."

It was true, and all his workers knew it. "No one has ever left my company, and no one ever will. Look at them, they'd jump from the top of St. Vitus' Cathedral if I ordered them," he boasted.

"Yes, Master, your servants would do anything for you," Zdenko agreed.

"Especially us," Zdenka added. "We'd do *anything* for you."

Zdenko cocked his head towards Zdenka. She wrinkled her brow. Until now, neither had confessed such devotion to anyone but the other. Zdenko loosened his collar, Zdenka twisted her plaits. They stared deep into each others eyes and smiled, awkwardly at first, then they linked arms. The tiny chink in their bond closed, as quickly as it had appeared.

"Excuse me, sir," called a tall boy. "I'm sorry to interrupt, but could you spare a few minutes to discuss tomorrow's rehearsal? I need to finish mapping the stage plan."

It was Karel, the Head Marionette-Maker, charged with designing and carving most of the marionettes for the new production. Plucked from a poor family, Karel had become the Master's apprentice two years ago. He had learned quickly and anyone who saw his work would have agreed that he was something of a puppeteering prodigy.

The Master swung to face him. "What's that?" he snarled. "Laddy-locks, I'd be the first to admit that you're no fool when it comes to carving creatures from wood, but I don't employ you to interfere. We'll discuss the rehearsal and stage plan in the morning, after you've distributed the last of the leaflets."

Back in his wagon, he seized his goblet of wine, took a great swig and pulled vigorously on his beard. "Everything's going to plan, but my principal preoccupation is to ensure my star performer remains hidden from prying eyes. No one but we three know where it is, and none but me has seen it. Without it there will be no transcendence of theatre, art, or history. Failure would mean being cursed to damnation by my ancestors. Their corpses will rise from their graves and drag me to hell."

"We won't tell anyone, Master, you can be sure of that. But how exactly are you going to transcend history?" asked Zdenko.

"I approve of your curiosity! Allow me to show you. Stand across the room. Both of you, that's it, as far as you can go. Turn around. Face me."

The twins positioned themselves at the end of the wagon, next to what the Master called his Cabinet of Cruelty. Zdenka thought it was the most beautiful thing she had ever seen. She touched the glass doors, desperate to examine the collection of stuffed rats, dried insects and rotten bird's eggs inside. "If only they were mine," she thought.

"Zdenka! Look this way," the Master ordered. "I demand your absolute attention." He pressed his thumb and index finger together and placed them on the bridge of his nose. He closed his eyes, opened them wide and gazed upwards. Then he locked his gaze upon the twins. Their neck bones cracked as their muscles relaxed and their heads fell, Zdenko's to the left, Zdenka's to the right.

"Raise your left hands. Now your right. Twirl like little hurricanes."

They did as the Master commanded.

"Zdenka, bring me more wine."

She swayed to the table and refilled the Master's goblet with an unsteady hand.

"Pass me that sword, Zdenko."

Zdenko walked stiffly to a chest of props, picked up the weapon, handed it jerkily to the Master.

"Splendid!" the Master appraised him. "My skills have risen to a magnificent crest." With a snap of his fingers, a flash of his eyes, he released the twins from their trance. They collapsed like rag dolls into the chest.

"What happened?" asked Zdenko. "I feel odd . . . wobbly in the head."

"Excellent," said the Master. "That's exactly how you're supposed to feel."

"What did you do?" asked Zdenka. "Was it a kind of ***witchcraft***?"

"You could say that. It's a form of mind manipulation, a means of controlling people, of willing them to execute your every command. You will shortly be initiated into the ways of the hypnotist yourselves, but now I must rest." The Puppet Master slumped into his armchair and, within moments, the wagon resounded to the rumble of his snores.

Zdenka knew he'd be dead to the world for at least a few hours so she opened the Cabinet of Cruelty and plucked a rat from the bottom shelf. ***"He'll never know,"*** her eyes gleamed as she put the stiffened creature into her pocket.

She crept from one corner of the wagon to another, wondering what other treats she might find. She opened his wardrobe. It was crammed with garish costumes – shiny capes, brightly embroidered waistcoats. She rummaged around, then pulled out three boxes, each the size of a biscuit tin. She opened the first.

"What's inside?" asked Zdenko.

"Just some straw, I think."

"Let me see," he replied, taking the box from Zdenka. There, beneath the straw, loosely wrapped in sackcloth, was a tiny wax model of a boy. A label had been pinned to his chest. It read:

'Work hard, work true,
work your skin through
Crafting the cast
will crumble your past'

"It looks like Karel," whispered Zdenka. Hurriedly, she opened the second box. It contained another two wax models, one male, the other female. "This must be you, and this is me! Here, take yours," she said to Zdenko, scrutinising the model of herself. "Even their clothes are like ours!"

"Look at the clever expression on this one's face," said Zdenko smugly. "And his laces are almost as neat as mine. But there's no note." He checked inside the tin, then picked up the third box. Zdenko tried to open it but it was nailed shut. A bronze plaque was fixed to the lid. The inscription read:

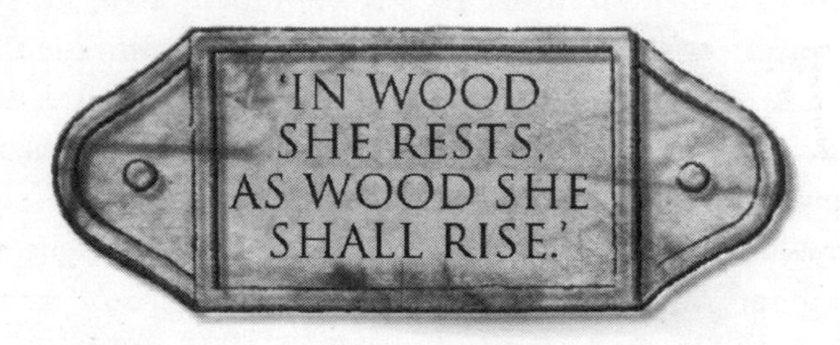

The Master grunted. He thrust back his head and grunted again. The twins waited until he had settled, then bundled everything back into the wardrobe. Stealthy as stoats, they left the wagon.

The Sound of her Blood

Milena had been lying in bed watching the shadows of the trees outside lurch across the floor for what seemed like hours, but had probably only been ten minutes, fifteen at most. Sleep was impossible. Certain that her dreams were signs of Libuse's legacy, she was more determined than ever to find her mother.

She climbed out of bed, shivering as her bare feet touched the floorboards. In the moonlight, she made her way to the bookcase. She struck a match and lit a candle. Her eyes scanned the shelves. There was a collection of fairy tales, an illustrated bestiary, a history of marionettes and a Czech-German dictionary. She pulled out a book called *Tales from the Rocking Chair.* It fell open at one of her favourite stories.

The Story of Wooden Otesanek

There was once a little old woman who had never been blessed with a baby of her own so her husband carved her a child from the roots of a tree. And the root came to life and sprouted fingers and toes, and a big round head that grew a shock of thick brown hair. The little old woman was delighted with her child and she named him Otesanek.

But Otesanek was an unusual boy. Everyone who met him agreed that he was the greediest child they had ever known. He ate and he grew, and he ate and he grew, and he ate and he grew even bigger and by the time Otesanek was two years old he was the size of a fully grown man. But he didn't stop there. He had to keep feeding his belly, which never seemed to fill, no matter how much he ate. He finished all the porridge and all the soup in his mother's kitchen. But he was still hungry. So he gobbled up his little old mother and his father. But he was still hungry. So he ran out to the fields and ate a girl and her wheelbarrow full of cabbages, a farmer and his field of corn, a shepherd and his flock of sheep. But he was still hungry. Then he saw an old lady, as wrinkled as a raisin, tending cabbages in her garden. But before Otesanek had chance to eat her, the old lady opened up his big, round belly with her hoe. Out popped the shepherd and his sheep, the farmer and his field of corn, the girl and her wheelbarrow full of cabbages, his father, his mother, all the soup and all the porridge.

And all that remained of greedy guts Otesanek was a shrunken tree root.

Milena looked around her room. Her bed along the far wall faced the window. In summer she left it open and fell asleep with a warm breeze tickling her cheeks. In winter she left a small space between the curtains so she could watch snow tumble from the sky. Milena had always preferred the colder seasons. When the first flurry of crunchy leaves fell from the trees, she knew it was time for her and Baba to visit Petrin Hill to pick juicy blackberries for pies and pancake fillings. They would wind their way to the top of the hill and eventually arrive at Petrin Tower which had been built for Prague's 1891 Jubilee Exhibition. If there was money to spare, Baba would buy them a snack from the refreshment stand and, once, they had even gone inside and climbed the two hundred and ninety nine steps that led to a viewing platform, from which it was possible, when the weather was fine, to see Snekza Mountain, the highest in all Bohemia.

Milena ran her fingers across the top of the bookcase, where she kept her most precious possessions – the stones she had collected on walks through the forest with her father, an acorn from the towering oak she had climbed with Lukas last summer, a galloping marble horse Aunt Tereza had given her a few birthdays ago.

Above the bed was a charcoal drawing of her father as a young boy, dressed in short black trousers and a high-collared white shirt. A marionette dangled over his left arm. Milena knew she would have to see lots more shows if she was going to reopen his theatre one day. She knew she had to find a way to meet the Puppet Master again. And she definitely had to see his show.

With this in mind, she pulled a trunk containing her favourite of Maminka's belongings from beneath her bed. She unfolded a bejeweled blue gown and held it up against her. She pulled out a pair of well-worn satin ballet shoes and slipped them on. They were too big but she tied their ribbons around her ankles and tried to stand en pointe. She tightened the muscles in her legs but no matter how hard she concentrated her knees kept trembling and she couldn't stay on her toes for more than a few seconds.

Further rummaging revealed a scrapbook of tickets and concert programmes carefully arranged in chronological order. Her mother's name had been written neatly on the cover and handwriting in the margins described why each item had been preserved. "My first solo performance, age twelve" next to a ticket, and a poster labelled "My favourite role - Sleeping Beauty". In most of the programmes she appeared on the bill as "Ludmila the Beautiful".

Tucked inside the back cover was a sheet of crimson card.

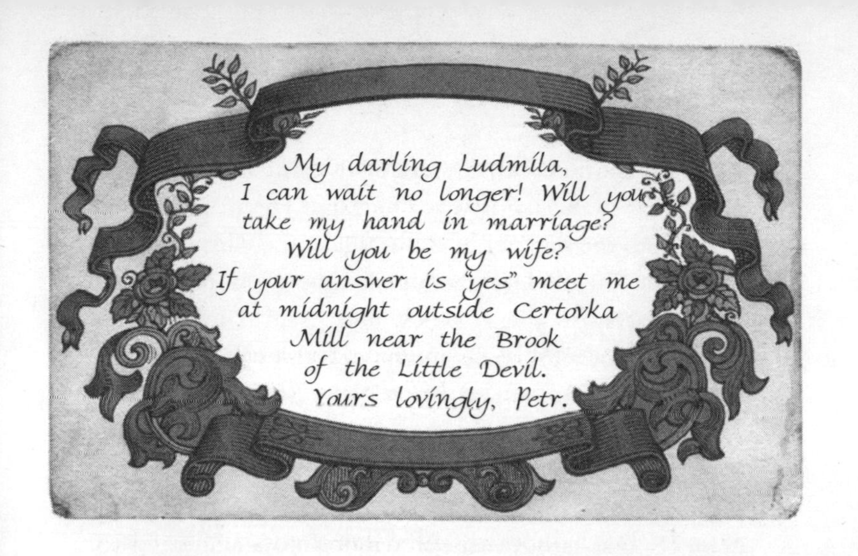

My darling Ludmila,
I can wait no longer! Will you take my hand in marriage?
Will you be my wife?
If your answer is "yes" meet me at midnight outside Certovka Mill near the Brook of the Little Devil.
Yours lovingly, Petr.

Milena picked up a corsage of roses. The petals crumbled at the edges. She ran the soft bristles of Maminka's ivory-handled hairbrush through her own unruly hair until it was smooth and free of knots. Near to the brush was something wrapped in a silk scarf. Milena pulled off the scarf and saw a jewellery box. She picked a ring and tried it on; a Czech garnet set upon a slim silver band. It fitted her middle finger perfectly. Gently, she polished the red stone with the sleeve of her nightdress.

But the treasure that delighted Milena most was the limewood marionette that lay across the bottom of the trunk, nestled on a bed of petticoats. Milena lifted her out, stroked the white fur trim that decorated the bottom of her dress. It was the only one of her father's creations not to have been buried with him, as was the custom for great marionette makers. She especially loved the marionette because it reminded her of both her parents.

"She's perfect!" She smelled a faint trace of her mother's rose and sandalwood perfume. Her tears fell like pearls onto the doll's cheeks. "You'll be the star when the House of Dream Delights opens again," she promised.

Milena lay in the darkness and strained to hear, in case her mother's voice might call through the wind that whistled and wailed down Novy Svet. Was that the sound of her heart? Was that the sound of her blood? Was that her laughter tinkling from the bell above the front door? Were those her fingers feeling through the branches that tapped on the window pane? She closed her eyes and saw Old Father Cech climbing the mountain to find a home for his people. She heard King Krok announce the birth of his firstborn, Kasa. She saw Libuse and her sisters walking through Vysehrad Castle gardens. She felt herself galloping through a forest on Libuse's white horse, a golden crown on her head, a pack of hunting dogs at her heels.

Then Milena saw Maminka running across Old Town Square. There she was, in the House of Dream Delights, kissing her husband for the last time. She saw a pair of gloved hands reach and grab her neck. A second pair clawed her clothes and hair. She saw her being dragged from the auditorium. She saw her father's body being covered in a white cloth. She heard a clatter of hooves. She saw shrouded figures flutter from the theatre.

"*Who are you*?" Milena screamed. She lay in a cold sweat, waiting for the morning to come, the din of hooves crossing cobblestones still pounding in her head.

Chamber of Hearts

The Master stirred in his sleep and knocked his goblet of wine to the floor. "Great blast from the gods!" he cursed. He tugged on his pocket-watch chain, squinted down at its white face. "The birds will be up within the hour."

He went to the wash basin, splashed his face with cold water. He caught sight of himself in the mirror. "The eyes of a beast, the eyes of a sovereign," he murmured. Little by little, he leaned closer until his nose touched the glass. "Is this not the face of a leader?" he asked his reflection. "Are these not the hands of a master?" He took a pace back, clenching his fists. "Yes," he declared, "they are."

He made his way across the wagon, opened his Cabinet of Curiosities and removed the panel that concealed a hidden compartment. It was divided into a dozen or so uniformly sized sections, in one a bundle of

human hair, in another a pair of satin ribbons. Here a pile of nail clippings, there a single mitten. The Master picked an object from the bottom corner. He stroked it tenderly, as if caressing a living creature. "I will not fail you, brother," he said, clutching the battered skull to his chest.

He flung open the wagon doors. "What a glorious night!" he said, gazing at the star-strewn sky. "But where did I put that key?" He searched his trouser and waistcoat pockets.

"Is this what you're looking for?" asked Zdenko from the bottom of the wagon steps.

The Master turned towards him with a start. "What are you doing here?" he barked, taking the key from Zdenko.

Zdenka emerged from beneath the wagon. "We thought you might need our assistance, Master," she smiled, flicking her tongue, serpent-like.

"Unbelievable. You're like each other's shadows. I have amassed many young apprentices over the years. Dozens have joined my theatre and danced to my tune, but none have ever shone with your luminosity. Have patience and you will understand everything. The others I set to work. The others are merely cogs in my well-oiled marionette-making machine but you, you are . . ."

"Indispensable?" suggested Zdenko.

"Humph," said the Master. "That may be so, but I need to be alone. Go home to your mother. You'll need your wits about you tomorrow."

At the back end of the wagon, he kneeled and felt for the door to his private chamber. He ducked, turned the key in the lock and pushed the door upwards. It creaked open and crashed down flat. He drew down a ladder and climbed inside.

The chamber was dark but the Master knew the layout well enough to manage without the aid of a candle, although he couldn't stand upright in the cramped room. It smelled of newly cut wood. Pieces of dusty velvet were draped over two of the walls. A table was littered with dismembered puppet heads and limbs, spare parts that might be used for future creations. There was a box displaying row after row of staring glass eyes, neatly laid out in order of size and colour. The Master felt his way along the workbench, stumbled over a rack of scuffed children's shoes. He stepped to the right.

There, strung from a series of rusty hooks, was a huddle of hanging bodies.

He smiled.

The row of freshly painted marionettes was charged with an energy that buzzed and fizzed around them. These particular puppets, his most prized, had been granted the privilege of travelling aboard his wagon while the rest of the cast hung in the carpenters' carts.

"Good evening, my darlings," the Master called to his menagerie. He smiled affectionately at Hag Woman, whose black and white striped apron reached to the floor. Her balding head was covered with a head scarf tied beneath her chin. A solitary tooth poked from her small round mouth.

Dangling next to her was the Lady of Barley. She carried a bag of oats in her right hand and pheasant feathers were stuffed into her apron pocket. Stumpy trotter-like hands curled at her sides.

The Master moved back and clapped his hands. "I trust you found the journey comfortable. We're here at last, and it's almost time for your first performance. I need not ask if you are ready."

As he spoke, the marionettes twisted their wooden necks to face him. A series of earsplitting creaks echoed around the chamber as, one by one, they bowed their heads. They loosened the joints in their shoulders, elbows and wrists, raised their arms and legs as the Master's presence gave them life.

"You are glad to see me, aren't you, my beauties? I'll take you outside tomorrow, and show you the stage, give you your instructions."

The chamber prickled with the clatter and clack of moving marionette limbs. The more attention the Master paid them, the more animated they became. Lady of Barley locked her hazel eyes on him and furiously pedalled her brown boots, showering the cage with feathers.

"It's as if your hearts beat with real blood, especially you, my beautiful beast," said the Master to his golden-horned Devil marionette. "How smart you look," he added, admiring the costume Madam Pinwoman had spent weeks perfecting.

Hairy-necked and two heads taller than his companions, Diablovich whipped the air with his fur-tipped tail. He kicked with the hoof on the end of his left leg, flexed the toes at the end of his right. The Master snapped his fingers and the marionette's eyes came to life. They blinked and flickered fast as flies' wings.

"I've thought of this moment since I was a young man," said the Master, fondly stroking Diablovich's tail, "and soon my decades of study will pay off. Nothing happens by accident. Everything happens by design. I need nothing but you, my wooden warriors."

He crouched and lowered his voice. "And how are you on this most enchanting night?"

There it was, his star. So protective was the Master of his most prized possession that he hadn't been content hiding it away in this secret room. That wasn't enough. It had also been installed in a cage. A small but secure iron cage which, if disturbed, would cause a bell to clang in his wagon. And here it was, seated on a straight-backed chair, dressed in shimmering red silk, unfastened from its strings, head to one side.

"Not answering me?" he whispered through the bars. "Maybe it's just as well; you need to conserve your energy. Sleep well, my beautiful caged bird. I shall see you tomorrow. Goodnight, my glittering star."

The Master manoeuvered his way back to the chamber entrance, climbed down the ladder, closed the door behind him.

"Hello, Master. Is everything all right?"

"Karel! What are you doing here?"

"I couldn't sleep, sir. I'm too excited about the show."

"Return to your wagon immediately. Go! Or do you want a beating?" The Master waited for Karel to cross the camp before the locking the chamber.

ACT TWO
Thursday 13th January, 1898

At the Place of Buttons and Boots

Milena opened the cottage door and felt a sudden a rush of excitement. Overnight the city had been covered by several feet of snow. As far as her eyes could see, Milena's world had become a glistening citadel of white. The bells of the Loreta Church began to chime as Milena walked up Novy Svet, pausing to step softly in the white patches that had not yet been trodden on.

Milena stopped at the edge of Castle Square, enthralled by what she saw. On clear starlit winter nights, or in the glowing amber of dawn, the Square was at its most beautiful, but now, encased in snow and ice, the palaces and convent which lined it, and the Castle itself – its gardens and courtyards, the apartments of state and St. Vitus' Cathedral – looked more spectacular than ever.

The hulking Giants in Combat statues – a chubby cherub astride a roaring lion, a colossus clubbing his cowering opponent – that guarded the Castle gates sparkled as if they'd been sculpted from crystal.

The Tale of the Loreta Bells

Long ago, in Prague's Castle District, there lived a widow whose children were known as the Loreta Bells, for the woman had as many children as there were bells in the church tower. When the Great Plague swept through the city, Death came and claimed her eldest child. The woman's only wealth was a string of silver coins each child had been given as a christening gift so she took one of the coins to the church and the largest bell tolled the death knell for her firstborn.

When the woman returned from the burial, her second born fell ill and died. She brought another coin to the church and again a bell rang the death knell. So it went on until all the woman's children had been taken from her. Immediately after burying her youngest child, the widow fell ill and died and there was no-one to pay for the tolling of her own death knell. But, suddenly and inexplicably, the bells began to ring of their own accord. And to this day, the people of Castle District think of the widow and her Loreta Bell children whenever they hear ringing from the church tower.

She continued across the icy Square to the Castle wall. Directly beneath her crouched hundreds of Mala Strana cottages, crooked and cramped, their red-tiled roofs the only colour in the expanse of white. She saw the spires of the Tyn Church and Petrin Hill. Looking south she saw as far as Vysehrad, where the horizon and whole world seemed to come to an end. She descended Nerudova Hill and turned right. There, at the end of the passageway, was the familiar rusty sign of Lukas' shop. A shop that sold everything.

A bell sounded as Milena stepped inside.

"Milena! How lovely to see you. No school this morning?" asked Lukas' father.

"I'm on my way now, but I need to speak to Lukas."

"I'm here!" said Lukas. "But why are you here?"

"Would you like to come to tea at my aunt's house this afternoon? Is that all right with you, Mr. Laskavy? Mr. Kolar will come to collect him."

"I'd love to, thanks Milena."

"I've got something to tell you, too." But before she could continue the doorbell jingled and a tall boy came into the shop.

"Can I help you?" asked Mr. Laskavy.

"I was wondering if I could leave these leaflets for

your customers," Karel said.

"An actor, are you?" asked Mr. Laskavy.

"Yes. I arrived last night with a travelling theatre company, but there aren't any actors in our show."

Milena watched the dark-eyed stranger walk to the counter and hand Mr. Laskavy a leaflet. She followed the tread of his handsome boots, gazed at his thick brown hair, his soft features.

"Hello," he said, smiling at her. Milena's cheeks began to burn. She dropped her gaze, pretending to be interested in a jar of pickled cucumbers. "Hello," she mumbled.

"What's all this then?" asked Mr. Laskavy. "What's this *Legends of the Future*? Do you know about it, Milena? You're our theatrical expert."

"It's a puppet theatre," replied Karel, "although if you were to see the marionettes and how my Master handles them you could be forgiven for thinking they're real people."

"Do you mean the show on Petrin Hill?" asked Milena, forgetting her embarrassment.

"Yes, that's the one. I'm Karel, the Head Marionette Maker."

Milena's heart beat faster. "I met the Puppet Master last night. Scary, isn't he?"

"Are you really the Head Marionette Maker?" asked Lukas.

"Yes, really." Karel turned back to Milena. "My Master can seem scary, he's not an easy man to work for, but he's a true artist, the best there is. Almost like a second father. Are you coming to the show?"

"I wish I was," sighed Milena, "I love marionette theatre. My mother was a dancer and my father a puppeteer. Have you heard of the House of Dream Delights? It had to close after he died but I'm going to open it again one day."

"Then you have to come, Milena," Karel insisted. "I could give you a tour of the showground, take you backstage. You could visit my workshop too."

Lukas glared at him.

"It will be a night you'll never forget," promised Karel, his eyes searching Milena's.

Lukas picked up one of his hand-carved flutes and blew a short blast of air through it.

"Lukas!" Milena cried. "We're talking."

"Sorry, just trying it out." He turned to Karel. "Did you want anything else? I'm sure you're very busy."

Karel laid a handful of coins on the counter, picked up two caraway seed rolls, a wedge of Moravian cheese and an apple. "I'll take these, please. It was nice to meet you all, but you're right, Lukas, I have got lots to do back at the camp. Hope to see you there soon," he said, looking again at Milena. "Promise you'll try and come."

"I will," she said as Karel left the shop. "Hope to see you again too."

"What a bighead! The show probably isn't *that* good," muttered Lukas. "And I still don't believe he's the chief puppet maker."

"Come on, Lukas. You saw the poster. It looked amazing. I could have talked to him about marionettes for hours."

"I don't see what all the fuss is about. There are dozens of marionette shows in the city. Why should this be more special than the others? But what's this news of yours?"

Milena shook her head. "I can't tell you now – there's no time! You'll just have to wait until this afternoon."

Karel made his way back to Petrin Hill, munching his apple as he went. The day was bright, he had delivered all the leaflets, and he was enjoying every moment of his first visit to Prague. Karel was confident the Master would have no cause to find fault with his work, and that his temper would calm when he saw the marionettes onstage and heard the audience's applause. Karel knew his parents would be proud of him. But, as he crunched through the snow, he realised that he couldn't recall the last time he'd thought of his family. He paused, trying to picture his father's face. But he couldn't. Instead he saw the Master. He tried to visualise his family's cottage in the country, but all he saw was the Master's wagon. He tried again, concentrated on imagining his younger brothers and sister playing in the orchard. He thought sadly of his mother laying his place at the kitchen table, lighting a candle for him before bed. The same happened again. He couldn't picture them.

"Why can't I see them?" Karel asked himself. "Why can't I remember what they look like? Has so much time passed?"

He thought of the day the Master had come for him, and the horrified look on his mother's face as he was bundled into the back of the Master's wagon.

Karel continued to his workshop to check his beloved horse marionette. He'd spent months carving it, and had even made several miniature versions before beginning work on this final life-size one. The mane and tail were real horse hair, the hooves shod so when it trod the boards of the stage they would clop authentically. He couldn't wait to see the Master bring his horse to life on the stage. He couldn't wait to see him make it rear and stretch like a galloping thoroughbred. Perhaps he would even be allowed to operate it himself one day, but he knew that for this show the Master had decided not to use any puppeteers. He had made it clear that he was going to control the marionettes himself.

Karel stroked the horse's mane, polished its glass eyes with the cuff of his shirt. It was perfect. Yes, his parents would be proud of him but, suddenly, a terrible feeling of guilt swelled in his belly. How could he have said the Master was like a second father to him? His real father had never even raised his voice, let alone his fists. "When will I see him again?" he wondered. "What if I never see any of them again?"

Long of Hair, Short of Sense

Miss Slovakova entered the classroom. Everyone stood. "Good morning, girls," she said briskly. "I hope you're feeling lively this morning. We're starting a new topic today. Milena, you can read first," she said, handing out copies of *The Myths and Legends of Ancient Bohemia*.

Chapter Two

The Ploughman King

For many years people rejoiced at the sight of Libuse riding through the land on her white horse, for her presence ensured their safety and fair treatment, but in time some began to resent being the only tribe led by a woman and, followingan incident involving two men disputing the boundaries between their land, the tribe was changed forever.

Unable to resolve their differences the men had no alternative but to go to their Queen. Libuse listened carefully to both and eventually ruled in favour of the younger man.

The older fellow was outraged. He thrust his walking stick into the ground and yelled, "What do women know of disputes between men? We all know that they are long of hair but short of good sense".

"You seem to confuse cruelty and brute force with justice," said Libuse calmly. "You do not recognise the gentle and considered practice of the justice of women. You only recognise leadership when it is delivered with a rod of iron. But tomorrow I shall gather the people

and ask them if they would prefer the rule of a man. If that is what they desire, I shall find a husband and he will rule over you." So saying, Libuse returned to her castle and the crowd dispersed.

Next day, just as the sun rose, a stream of people came to the Queen's castle. The higher it rose, the bigger the crowd became, until at last Libuse emerged from her chamber. "What have you decided? Do you wish to exchange my rule for that of a man?" she asked.

The crowd were unanimous. "Yes! Yes!" they all shouted.

"Very well, my people, but I ask you not to forget that while it is easy to seat a prince upon the throne, it is very difficult to remove him. But, since you have made up your minds, I can tell you where you will find your leader."

The crowd cried out, "We want a Prince, we want a Prince!"

Libuse raised her right hand towards the mountains and called out, "Beyond these mountains runs a river. Along its banks you will find a village called Stanice. My horse will lead you inland from this village to a piece of land being ploughed by a man and two striped oxen. One of the animals will have a white head and a white stripe on its front, while the other will have a white forehead, back and hind legs. The man will be brown of hair and soft of features. He is Premsyl the

Ploughman and will be my husband and rule over you. Take this robe and these fine boots and present them to him, for these signify the arrival of his regal role."

Libuse's horse was brought in front of the castle and it led the crowd through a forest which came out onto a plain overlooked by the mountain Rip. The horse followed the path of the river until it reached Stanice. The crowd turned and saw a man ploughing a field with two oxen, one with a white head and a white stripe on its front and the other with a white forehead, a white back and white hind legs, all exactly as Libuse had described.

"All hail Premsyl! All hail our chosen Prince!"

The ploughman stopped working and the entourage told him he had been chosen by Queen Libuse to be her husband, and their King. Saying nothing, Premsyl unharnessed the oxen and they lumbered off. He struck the hazel wand he had been using to drive them and three branches growing leaves and nuts sprouted from it. Then he reached into his bag, took out some bread and cheese and invited the messengers to eat with him. As they ate together two branches of the hazel wand withered and died while the third grew stronger and stronger.

Observing the crowd's astonishment, Premsyl took hold of the hazel wand and said, "This branch is my tribe. Though it sprouts many masters only one will reign. But it is a shame that you found me so soon,

men. Had you come when I had finished ploughing this field there would never have been want in Bohemia. There would have been enough bread for everyone, forever."

The new King of Bohemia put on the robe and boots the crowd had brought for him and picked up his old worn sandals.

"Why are you bringing those old shoes with you, Master?" asked one of the crowd. "You have new boots which are far more suitable for the feet of a King."

"I am taking them with me so my descendants will not forget where they came from." So saying he mounted Libuse's horse and led the crowd back to her castle where a wedding feast was already being prepared. Libuse came out to greet her husband. "Hail the new King, my husband! May you reign long and fair!"

"Thank you, Milena, we'll finish there for today," said Miss Slovakova. "Girls, your homework is to read the next chapter."

Milena closed *The Myths and Legends of Ancient Bohemia*. "Why did they betray Libuse for a stranger? What will become of her?"

As she slipped the book into her satchel she thought of Premsyl and remembered Karel. He had seemed so clever. And handsome. She really hoped she would meet him again.

They Emerged from the Ether like a Pair of Ghouls

The auditorium of the Master's theatre was nearly assembled. The stage had been erected that morning, the scenery rigged, the musicians' places arranged in the orchestra pit. And now the last of the seats were being installed in the upper circle. A team of men were busy lining the walls and ceiling with velvet drapes, wheeling scaffolding into each corner then securing the material with nails. Madam Pinwoman and her girls had painstakingly sewn hundreds of sequins onto the ceiling drapes, giving the impression that the stars themselves had been brought into the auditorium.

Onstage Karel was taking the technicians through the opening scene.

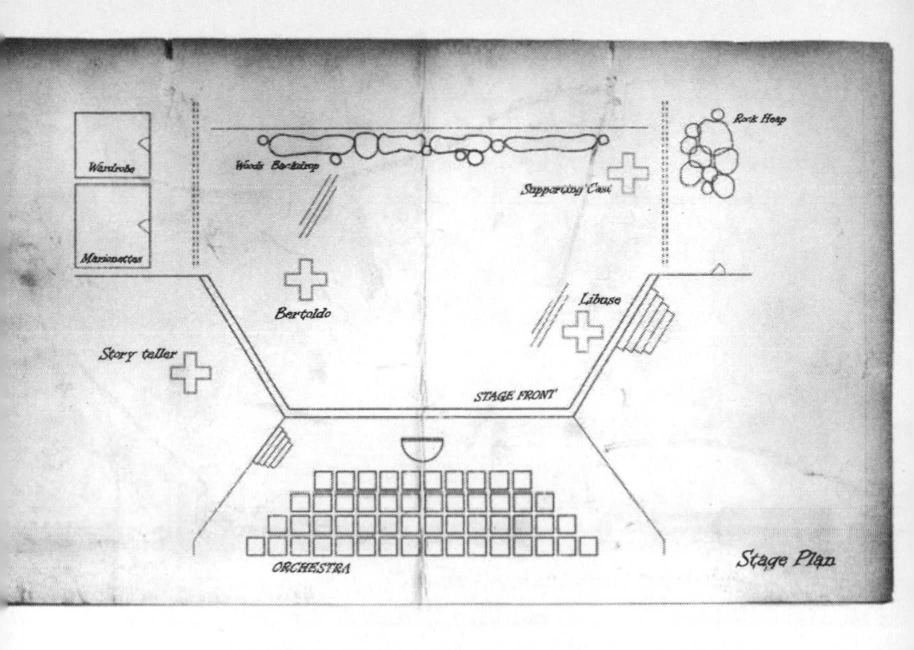

"As soon as the timpani drum is struck, the first set of curtains will be raised to reveal the forest. Green lights will illuminate the stage gradually and cast the shadows of trees across the boards. The Story-teller marionette will take his position here in the centre of a spotlight . . . " Karel strode across the stage and marked the Story-teller's position with a blue chalk cross. "The marionette will stop precisely on this spot. If he's even just a fraction off it we'll run into all kinds of trouble when the other characters are lowered. Zdenko! Zdenka!" he called. "Where are you? Is the Story-teller in costume?"

"Yes, Karel, the Story-teller is ready," said the twins in unison as they slipped onstage.

"Never one, is it? Always two," sighed Karel, nervously eyeing them up and down. "Where did you come from?"

"First we were there," said Zdenka, pointing to the wings.

"And now we are here," added Zdenko, winking at his sister.

"Like a pair of ghouls emerging from the ether," Karel muttered under his breath.

"Ghouls?" repeated Zdenka. "Ghouls? We're sorry, Karel. We don't mean to alarm you," she smirked.

"Yes, we didn't mean to alarm you," said Zdenko flatly. "The Story-teller is ready."

"Don't be ridiculous," Karel replied, shifting uncomfortably. "I wasn't alarmed."

He may have been older than them, but the twins' presence never failed to disturb him. Their unfathomable language of blinks and twitches, their eerie ability to appear from nowhere; there was something otherworldly about them.

"What do you want us to do with him?" asked Zdenka. "Shall we bring him on?"

"No, one of the stagehands will fetch him. I don't want anything to go wrong."

"But what could possibly go wrong . . . ?" Zdenka purred.

". . . not when the Master has entrusted us with so much important information," finished Zdenko.

Karel froze. "What information? I'm in charge of the marionettes."

"That may be so, but there are certain things, certain special things you don't know," Zdenka taunted, deriving great pleasure from Karel's distress. "Like where the main marionette is hidden."

"Would you mind leaving the stage?" Karel asked, struggling to conceal his anger and disappointment. After last night he thought he had a good idea as to where it was being kept, but that wasn't the point. The Master should have trusted him.

"Perhaps we do mind, Karel. Perhaps we don't." Zdenka rolled her eyes towards her brother. He screwed up his nose in reply.

The twins swept off the stage leaving a cloud of arrogance trailing behind them. They placed themselves next to their mother and looked on as the Story-teller marionette was hoisted into position, then fixed onto the platform high above the stage. A group of stage technicians extended its body down until its wooden feet touched the chalk cross. Karel breathed a sigh of relief. It was the first time he'd seen any of the marionettes in costume onstage.

"Would you tell the musicians they are needed? Twins?"

"We're right behind you," said Zdenko. "You can never know where and when we might appear."

"And, as if by magic, the musicians are already on their way." Zdenka added, casting a fleeting glance at the orchestra pit.

"Technicians, dim the lights!" Karel ordered. "Music please!"

The cellists took up their bows and began to play a deep, penetrating drone overlaid with an ascending run of violin notes, bowed slowly and lightly. And then the first timpani sounded and rumbled through the star-lit, green hued auditorium, cueing the raising of the curtains. The Story-teller descended with a nod of his shaggy-grey-haired head. Madam Pinwoman's face flushed with satisfaction when she saw how perfect his costume looked. He held a walking stick and wore a tunic with a bronze-buckled belt around the middle. Madam Pinwoman's feather jutted from his felt hat.

Karel held his breath as the Story-teller's feet touched the ground and, starkly lit by a spotlight, he struck his stick onto the stage with a crack. The marionette's jaw clacked up and down.

"Ladies and Gentlemen, may I welcome you most heartily to this Show of Shows . . ."

"One, two . . ." murmured Zdenko under his breath. On the count of three the Puppet Master swept into the auditorium. Karel paled as the twins positioned themselves either side of him. How could they have known he was approaching?

"How's the rehearsal going?" asked the Master, placing a cold hand on the back of Karel's neck.

"Well, I think."

"Is that right, twins? He's not hiding anything from me, is he? No secrets? No disasters?"

"He does seem jumpy," Zdenka replied.

"Nervous, even," added Zdenko.

"No one can fault my work. I can assure you of that. The performance will run like clockwork," Karel promised.

"Good. That is, after all, what you're here for. But we cannot afford to be lazy. Like an old wolf, I will not rest until these paws are gripping success by the throat. Don't delay proceedings. Get on with it."

The Master turned to Zdenko and Zdenka. "The time has come." He shepherded them to a dark recess at the back of the auditorium. "Did you check the ticket sales?"

Zdenka's face contorted into a self-satisfied smile. "We did, and we've already sold most of the tickets for the first week. There are only a few seats left."

"Excellent, just as it should be. Gather closer. What I am about to impart is for your ears only."

The Master stooped low, whispered the twins their instructions. "Is that understood?" he asked. "In the name of Bertoldo's bones, you must follow these orders exactly."

The twins nodded. Unseen, they slipped out of the auditorium, itching with excitement.

Down to the Cellar

At last the bell sounded and school was over. Milena dashed outside, climbed into Mr. Kolar's carriage and they began their journey through the snow-clad city. Her eyes followed the flakes that swirled like hundreds of miniature whirlwinds. As they crossed Karluv Bridge the snowfall thickened and she couldn't see beyond the statues. She gazed up in the direction of the castle. Like the Vltava River, it too had vanished in a cloud of powdery ice.

"We're almost there now," Mr. Kolar called from the driver's seat. "Whoa!" He tugged on the reins. The horse steadied to a trot, then stopped with a nod of its head.

Standing in the shop doorway, Lukas saw them arrive and ran outside. "Hello Milena," he grinned as he got into the carriage, brushing snowflakes from his hair. "You weren't late for school, were you? Sorry I was so

bad-tempered this morning. I don't know what I was thinking."

"That's all right," Milena smiled. "You're forgiven. So, do you want to hear my news?"

After telling him about Baba's revelation Milena waited for Lukas' response, but none came. "Well, say something!" she giggled. "You look like a fish with your mouth hanging open. I think you should start calling me Your Highness from now on."

"Very funny, Milena, but I don't believe a word of it."

"It's true! Baba told me everything last night. You can ask her yourself."

"She really told you that? Are you sure it wasn't a dream, or perhaps you've taken one of her tales too seriously? Or maybe you're just playing a trick on me."

"I'm not making it up. It's all true. I'm a descendent of the very first Queen of Bohemia. Someone has to be, I suppose, so why shouldn't it be me? And today at school we started reading a book about the ancient legends of Bohemia and everything matched what Baba told me."

The sunlight began to fade and the last drops of warmth were squeezed from the afternoon as the carriage turned onto Vinohradska Street and clattered into the cobbled courtyard of the House of the Ladies of the Snow.

"It's wonderful to see you!" cried Tereza. She threw her arms around Milena and Lukas and hugged them both tightly. "You look more like your mother every time I see you, Milena. You have the same lovely hair, her sparkly green eyes. And Lukas, you're looking every inch a handsome young man. Come, I've laid out a feast."

Inside, the dining table was covered in a lace cloth and the finest silverware. In the centre of the table, on a three tiered stand, was a selection of sugar-dusted coffee and vanilla babovka cakes, slices of apple strudel and fruit pancakes.

"I need to talk to you about something," said Milena, once she and Lukas had helped themselves to cups of hot chocolate and slices of babovka. "Last night Baba told me all about Father Cech and King Krok and Libuse and her white horse, and how our family is descended from her family. Then at school today I learned about her husband, King Premsyl . . . "

"At last you know!" Tereza exclaimed. "I've always known you'd inherited your mother's intuitions, but we must see if you have my gifts too, Milena. I'll fetch some of my herbs so we can find out."

"What gifts? Can you see into the future too? Why do you need herbs?"

"Herbs are the origins of medicine, my dear. They're for remedies, healing ointments, restorative charms, that kind of thing. In the days before tablets and bottled medicine and clinics and hospitals, wise women made sick people well and warded off danger through their knowledge of plants. Did Baba tell you about Libuse's sisters?"

"Yes, she did." Milena tried to recall what Baba had said about them. "I think I understand," she smiled. "You're like Teta, aren't you, Tereza? And Katerina, you're a doctor, which is what Kasa the Healer would be if she were alive today. Will you show me one of your spells? I must know *everything* Libuse and her sisters knew."

"Milena, you must realise that the gifts aren't a game," Katerina cut in. "Did Baba tell you how difficult it was for your mother?"

Milena nodded.

"In that case you'll understand that the gifts that accompany the legacy be used wisely."

"Then let me show Milena how to use the gifts responsibly, Katerina." Tereza picked up her *Diary of Herbal Experimentation*. "Look at this," she said, flicking through the book. "It holds centuries worth of wisdom." She peeled a piece of horehound off a page. "For example, this little sprig can clear your mind and sharpen your senses. It can even quicken recovery from a fever."

"Are you sure a dry old leaf can do all that?" asked Milena.

"Indeed it can. But let's try something else. Read the last entry in my diary. The one about henbane. Now follow me."

In the kitchen Tereza tied a scarf around the bottom half of her face, put on a pair of gloves and picked a piece of henbane from a jar on a shelf in the pantry. She ushered Milena and Lukas outside while Katerina looked on from the back door.

"Do as I've done – cover your mouths and noses. You mustn't inhale the fumes." She struck a match and, holding the henbane at arms length, set it alight. Sparks blew around the garden. "Now, wait."

Milena looked at Lukas. She hoped something would happen soon.

"Patience, Milena." The stars disappeared behind a patch of clouds that had suddenly gathered directly overhead. A few drops of rain began to fall. "Here it comes . . . Watch out!"

Accompanied by a rumble of thunder, the clouds burst their seams and those few drops swelled to a heavy downpour. Within moments the garden path overflowed with water. Lightning flashed, striking the fir trees and stone wall with blinding streaks of electricity.

"You see!" Tereza's scarf-muffled voice rose over the din of the rain. "The power of henbane has been released!"

Milena looked up at the cluster of clouds. The rain smarted on her cheeks. She noticed that no rain fell in the garden next door, that the neighbour's trees were still and dry.

"Tereza!" called Katerina. "I think you've demonstrated your abilities, come inside before you all catch terrible colds."

"That was impressive!" said Lukas, shaking his head,

spraying the kitchen with rain water. "Never seen anything like it." He shut the door. The storm subsided as quickly as it had started.

"Yes, that is one of Tereza's showier skills. Traditionally used to help farmers in times of drought," Katerina explained.

While Katerina and Lukas were talking, Tereza led Milena from the kitchen.

"Where are we going?" asked Milena.

"To the cellar," Tereza whispered. "To continue your first lesson in herb-working."

"It's like a cavern," said Milena as she reached the bottom of the steps.

"This is my apothecary's den. It's where I prepare my herbs and brew my potions." Tereza struck a match, illuminating the cellar with a quiver of candlelight. "I've been waiting to bring you here since you were a little girl. Follow me."

The room was warm and smelled of earth. In the centre was a long bench covered in pestles and mortars, blocks of charcoal, candles and sachets of dried plants. Three of the walls were covered by cupboards packed with hundreds of jars of seeds, herbs, powders and oils. The fourth was lined with shelves that creaked beneath the weight of dozens of old books with titles like *Secrets of the Runes*, *Magic, Alchemy and Anima Mundi* and *Divination by Tarot*.

"Each of these pots and bottles contains a little piece of magic," Tereza explained. She opened a cupboard, took out a bundle of birch twigs and passed one to Milena. "For example, if you tie a red ribbon around this little stick and keep it about your person it will rid you of the evil eye. It's said witches made their brooms from the same branches. They called it Lady of the Woods." She squeezed Milena's arm. "In time, you will understand all this. It will become as second nature to you as it was to Libuse, Teta and Kasa. You're already as strong as Vlasta, and as beautiful as Sarka."

"Who are they?" asked Milena.

"Other women from the days of Libuse. I'll tell you their tales soon. You can't learn everything in a single night!"

Tereza lit three more candles. The cellar filled with the smell of burning candlewick. She took a fresh piece of henbane from a jar and tied it up in a handkerchief. "Take this as a reminder of what is possible. But never touch it with bare hands, never inhale the fumes, and never, ever ingest it. In short, treat it with the utmost care and caution. It has many uses, for example, wearing it about your person will attract love!"

Saying nothing, Milena placed the handkerchief in her pocket.

"You're very quiet. Is something troubling you?" asked Tereza.

"No," replied Milena. "I mean yes. But no one will believe me."

"I'll believe you."

"Maminka needs me. I think she's in danger. I've

dreamed of her every night since she went, but my dreams are becoming more and more frightening. Last night was the worst. It's as though I'm seeing through her eyes. I felt hands reach and pull at her clothes, as if they were grabbing *my* neck and pulling *my* clothes. Then I noticed figures flying away from the theatre, and there was a strange noise, like goats clambering over rocks, or maybe they were horses. Do you think she's trying to tell me something?"

Tereza stifled her alarm. "I think this happens because you love her so much, because you think of little else apart from her," she explained. "You may be Libuse's ancestress and Ludmila's daughter, but you also need to be yourself. I'll prepare some special remedies to help you, and I think you deserve a treat of some kind. Maybe we could visit Karlovy Vary or Cesky Krumlov for a few days. A trip to the countryside would do you good."

"Well, there is something I'd like," Milena replied. "I bumped into a Puppet Master on Old Town Square last night, and this morning I met his Head Marionette Maker. I'd love to see their show."

"Then you shall! Katerina and I have tickets for the opera tomorrow evening, so why don't we go on Saturday? Baba and Lukas must come too. I can't remember the last time we went on an excursion together. But I'm afraid we'll have to leave your lessons for tonight. It's getting late."

"Thank you!" Milena ran to the kitchen where

Katerina and Lukas were still talking. "Tereza said we could see the new marionette show on Saturday! You too, Lukas."

"Wonderful idea," replied Katerina. "What do you think, Lukas? I'll buy the tickets tomorrow."

Lukas glanced at Milena, then turned to Katerina. "I'd love to, thank you." He did want to see the show, but was in no hurry to see Karel again. He didn't want anyone to come between him and Milena, especially not an arrogant puppet-maker.

"Before you go, each take a piece of this horehound," Tereza insisted. "Place it in a cup of boiling water and drink the liquid to stay alert, or keep it in your pockets to protect you from sorcery, although I've never had to use it for such a peculiar purpose," she laughed. "Hurry along now, Baba will be waiting. Make sure Milena gets home safely, won't you, Lukas?"

Tereza closed the door behind them and turned to Katerina. "I have an uneasy feeling about something Milena said. I'll be in the cellar if you need me."

Dropped from the Tower

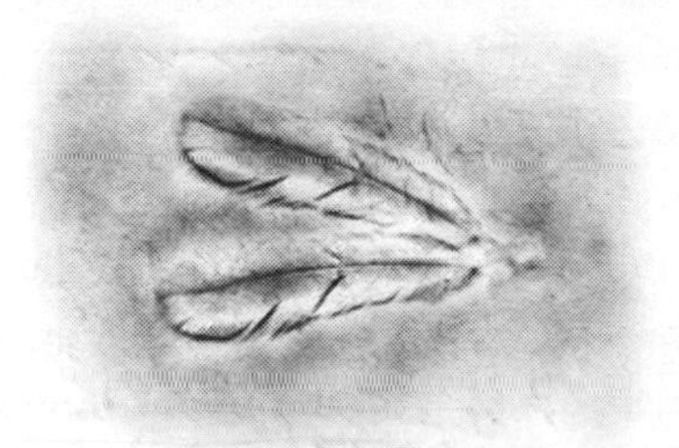

Milena and Lukas hurried home. The snow lay soft and thick on the ground. The moon was high and seemed brighter than the sun as it streamed down onto the Old Town and touched the roofs sharp with beams of silver and white. They approached the gateway to Lesser Quarter, passing tall narrow houses, dark-beamed inns and church spires that seemed to brush the stars. Milena felt like a tiny doll treading through a giantess' kingdom.

High above them, something stirred at the top of the Bridge Tower. Two figures ducked beneath the battlements.

"At last!" hissed Zdenka as Milena and Lukas stepped directly beneath the tower. She picked up a mirror and a piece of slate and began to scrape them together. The sound of stone grinding against glass echoed around the Vltava valley. Each stroke created a noise more

excruciating than its predecessor.

Zdenko pulled on a pair of gloves and dipped his fingers into a pail of sticky feathers. He pulled out a handful and sprinkled them over the battlements.

"What's that?" asked Milena, covering her ears. "And look! It's snowing again."

"That's not snow," said Lukas as a flurry of feathers cascaded around them.

While Zdenko emptied his bucket, Zdenka gathered a fistful of glass eyes from her bag. Leaning as far as was safe over the edge, she hurled the gleaming globes from the battlements. Splinters of coloured glass shot in all directions as the eyes smashed onto Karluv Bridge.

Revelling in the spectacle of Lukas and Milena cowering on the bridge below, Zdenka tugged Zdenko's sleeve. This wasn't exactly what the Master had instructed them to do. She was taking things further. Much further. "More!" flashed Zdenka's eyes. "More!"

Zdenko pulled a catapult from his back pocket, took aim and struck the statue of St. John Nepomuk clean on its star-capped crown. He reloaded his catapult and launched an even more aggressive attack. The eyes hurtled through the air at alarming speed.

Milena looked up to see where they were coming from. She felt a sharp stinging on her cheek. She cried out in pain.

"What do you think you're doing?" she yelled furiously. "How dare you?"

Zdenko tossed a rope over the edge of the tower. He lowered it until the basket attached to its end touched the ground.

Lukas ran towards it.

"No!" shouted Milena. "It might be best to leave it."

But Lukas couldn't help himself. He bent down and peered into the basket. There, lying face up on an old shawl was a rat, its jaw frozen open, its front teeth protruding like tiny bone daggers. Horrified, Lukas kicked it aside.

"What is it?" asked Milena.

"Nothing. Just a raggedy old shawl."

"It doesn't look like a shawl."

Milena grabbed the basket. She shuddered. "Why would anyone do this to us?"

Lukas shrugged. "Are you sure you're all right? You'll have a bruise tomorrow." He scooped up some snow and packed it into a tight ball. "This will help the swelling," he said, pressing it onto Milena's cheek.

She flinched, then took a deep breath. "I'm fine. Let's go home."

The twins watched their victims disappear from view and squeezed each others hands. They scurried down the tower's winding staircase two steps at a time. Like well-oiled mechanical toys, they moved swift and clean through the snow slicked passageways of the Lesser Quarter. Their spiky silhouettes looked as if they had been cut from thin pieces of iron. The pitter-patter of their little black shoes echoed through the empty streets.

They felt ready for anything. They felt ready to take on the world.

The Founding of the Threshold and a Cradle for a Crown

Baba was asleep in her rocking chair when Milena said goodbye to Lukas on the cottage doorstep. She tiptoed to her room with a candle and placed it on the floor near her bed. She paced around her room, shaken by the attack, tormented by a sense of foreboding. So many questions, and none could be answered. She slipped beneath her blankets, sat Maminka's marionette beside her on the pillow and opened *The Myths and Legends of Ancient Bohemia*. She forced herself to read.

Chapter Three

The City of Gold

Under the rule of proud King Premsyl the tribe founded by Brother Cech flourished. Forests retreated before fields, and between the fields hard-working hands built settlements and fortresses and farms. Harvests were bountiful and hunting expeditions always successful. The people were satisfied with their King and Libuse continued to use her gift of prophecy for the good of the people.

As the seasons rolled – spring, summer, autumn and winter – then span again into spring, the tribe swelled fourfold, fivefold, then six- and sevenfold and Libuse advised King Premsyl to find more land for his people. She suggested that he lead them to places where the earth was rich, where water ran clean and clear. She told him to seek land where the air was fresh, where forests would provide wood to build homes for shelter and fires for warmth. Following Libuse's advice, Premsyl's people wanted for nothing as they spread and settled where the four elements existed in harmony.

One evening the King and his Queen visited

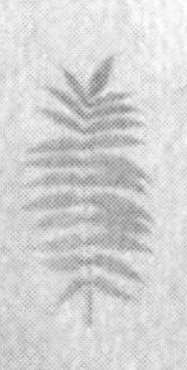

Libusin Castle. And as they sat on their horses at the highest point of the castle and looked across the glowing landscape, Libuse turned towards the shadows of the advancing evening and raised her arm towards the east. Everything fell silent. The birds ceased singing, the wind stopped rushing through the trees. Libuse placed her slender fingers on the bridge of her nose, let her arm fall and began to speak.

"Husband, I can see the future of our people. In the valley of those seven great hills, huddled around the Vltava River, I see a glorious city built in the shadow of a great castle. The castle perches high on a hill. It watches over the city like a strong sentry. You cannot yet see it, but this will be a place of wealth and wonder, a City of Gold, a place where no one will want for anything.

"Husband, travel to these hills at dawn. There you will see a man hewing a threshold. Where this man hews is the place the castle must be built. And this place shall be called Prague, which means threshold."

At sunrise Premsyl and his company of men journeyed towards the hills according to Libuse's directions. They came to the valley of the seven hills and rode through a forest until they happened upon a man hewing a threshold. Everything was as Libuse had foreseen and Premsyl and his entourage began building immediately.

News spread fast that Premsyl was founding a city of gold on the banks of the Vltava, in the valley of the seven hills. And the name Prague came to mean not only "threshold" but also splendour and wealth, for whoever lived there was blessed with unimaginable riches.

Libuse also saw deep into the earth and divined that gold could be found at Jilove and silver at Kutna Hora. In her time there was such an abundance of precious metals and gems that all the people wore jewellery fashioned from them. It was said that silver sprouted from the earth like wild flowers, that gold could be pulled from the ground like potatoes from a field. One piece of gold was so enormous that it weighed more than Libuse and Premsyl together. The King instructed his men to fashion an idol from this piece of gold so he and Libuse could offer sacrifices before it, so they could give thanks to the land for providing their people with such riches.

But danger still lurked in the forests, and none was more terrifying than the threat from one particular boar. His trotters were twice the size of human hands and the bristly brown hairs which spiked up in a ridge along his spine were sharp as swords. This King of Boars had made a den near the gates of Vysehrad and had grown so bold that he feared nothing. He would charge at hunting parties, strip dogs' flesh to the bone, rip men to shreds as if they were no bigger than mice.

No one knew how they could rid themselves of this menace, no one dared approach him. No one, that is, except for one brave young man called Bivoj.

Bivoj had long been in love with Kasa, Libuse's oldest sister and, determined to win her heart, he decided to track down the boar, for surely she would be unable to resist the charms of a handsome hero who had saved Premsyl's people from terror and death? Bivoj camouflaged himself, hid in a patch of bushes and observed the beast's habits for a week. He noticed that the boar rested in the same clearing at the same time every day so, armed with a wooden club and sharpened knife, Bivoj left his hiding place and set off for the clearing, planning to kill the boar while he slept. But, as fate would have it, on this particular day the boar wasn't in his normal resting place and while Bivoj wondered what to do the boar charged at him from behind. He heard the pounding of trotters and knew he had to act fast. He turned and raised his wooden club then smacked it down on the creature's head. The boar fell to the ground with an almighty thud. Bivoj bound the beast's feet together, slung it over his broad back and strode towards Vysehrad.

Libuse and Kasa were walking in the royal gardens when their conversation was suddenly interrupted by the cries of a cheering crowd. They rushed to the fortress gates to see what the noise was about. And the first thing they saw was Bivoj, marching towards them

with the boar snorting and writhing on his back.

Now Kasa's attention was guaranteed, Bivoj took his knife and cut the boar's throat before her. Kasa was so taken with Bivoj's bravery and strength that she agreed to marry him immediately. Naturally, the main dish of their wedding feast was the boar, the biggest, boldest beast Bohemia has ever known, and also the tastiest.

It came to pass that Libuse and Premsyl were blessed with a son and he was named Nezamysl. He lay in a golden cradle and was a kind and gentle child. But as soon as Nezamysl was strong enough to lift his father's sword, Libuse began to make preparations for her passing.

One evening she dressed herself in a purple robe, picked a linden branch from her garden and bade her maidens follow her to the river below Vysehrad. She asked them to throw the golden cradle into the deep black water. As her eyes followed its passage to the bottom of the river bed, Libuse saw the centuries that were to come. She saw times of prosperity and she saw times of terrible darkness and sorrow.

"Bury yourself!" Libuse called to the cradle. "Rest in the river bed and one day you shall rise from these waters, purified by tears of anguish, cleansed by the passing of time. And on that day, hands will grasp you and lay within you a child who shall restore goodness and peace to this land."

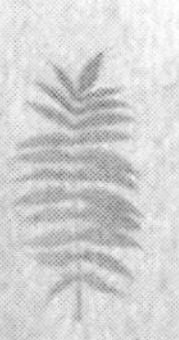

Libuse's eyes began to fail and she could hardly distinguish between the trees and the cliffs, but in the distance she saw Prague's glory begin to shine. She saw a city whose spires reached to the heavens, a city whose people were strong and proud and resilient, a city whose greatness and beauty was admired in all four corners of the world. She raised her linden branch and pointed towards the place where her City of Gold would grow.

"My time might be drawing to an end, but my people shall not perish. They shall triumph over all tribulations," she whispered. The branch fell from her hand onto the grassy cliff edge.

Libuse's maidens called for Premsyl and he came and carried his wife to her chamber. As those closest to her gathered around her deathbed, Libuse warned her husband of dangers that lay in the future. She thanked her maidens. She blessed her son. She slipped quietly away from this world. But it is said that the spirit of the great Queen rises from the soil whenever her people or land need her.

Milena put the book down and blew out the candle. Just as her eyes closed she heard a noise on the lane. The scuffling of shoes. The swish of a cloak. The sound of something whipping the air.

There was a light tapping on her window.

Tap-tap. Tap.

At once, terror came rushing back. She pulled her blankets around her.

Tap-tap-tap.

Tap-tap.

Milena mustered all her strength and crept across the room. She peeped through the curtains. She retreated in horror.

Puppets are Power, Legends are the Future

Milena's heart beat hard in her chest. She crouched on her bedroom floor beneath the window, wondering if she'd imagined what she'd seen.

She stood and pushed the curtains aside. She had been right. There, standing directly outside her bedroom window was a pair of identical twins, their faces pale, their expressions unfathomable.

Milena stared hard into their eyes. She opened the window. "Who are you . . . ?" She tried to hide the tremor in her voice. "What do you want?"

"We haven't come to answer your questions," scoffed Zdenko. "The Master says you're to have this." He reached through the window and passed Milena a golden envelope. She winced as Zdenko brushed against her arm. His fingers felt like chicken bones in his feather- and glue-covered gloves.

Zdenka grinned a crooked grin. "I see your cheek is still beautifully rosy."

"It was you!" Milena cried. "Why . . . ?"

"Be quiet," Zdenka interrupted. "We've brought you a present."

Milena looked at the wooden casket the girl had given her. There were tiny holes around its edges. "What's this?" she called. "Why have you come here?"

No answer came. They twins had already turned to leave.

"Wait! Come back!" she called after them. "Who are you?"

As she watched them slip away Milena noticed a third figure, less stealthy and much taller than the twins. She noticed something hanging from the back of its waist. Something that flicked of its own accord.

"How curious." She leaned out of the window, hoping to get a better view. But too late. The three figures had gone.

Milena closed the window, drew the curtains, sat on the end of her bed. She read the inscription. *In Wood She Rests, as Wood Shall She Rise.*

She removed the lid with trembling hands. Inside was a wax doll with a crumpled piece of paper tied to its left hand.

But that wasn't all. Milena opened the envelope. "What on earth . . . ?!" Inside the envelope were two tickets to the opening night of *Legends of the Future*. She looked at the doll again. It had long dark hair, a pale thin face, green eyes. And it wore a bright red coat. "It's me!" she gasped.

Still shaking, Milena climbed into bed, willing her mother and Libuse to send her a sign. "Do you know why I've been given these things?" she asked. "And what does the message mean?"

But, sign or no sign, Milena knew she had to overcome her fear. And she knew she had to attend the opening night of the show. "How else will I find out why such strange things keep happening?"

She stared at the doll for a long, long time, until at last her eyes closed and she fell asleep, still clutching it.

Sleep brought no peace. Milena found herself in the House of Dream Delights again, her father was at work.

Milena stirred. When she began to dream again, she was somewhere else. Somewhere green and cold and misty. And through the mists she saw a girl walking through a marsh. The girl was moving away from her. She was gliding towards what looked like a bustling

marketplace. She looked weightless, as if she were floating above the marshland. She stretched out her hands, parted the fog and hastened to the heart of the crowd. All of a sudden, one voice rang above the laughter and chatter.

"Remember that you are the blood of my blood and that your blood is the blood of this land."

Then came a deafening noise. The sound of hundreds of gulls flapping and screaming. And then the thunder of hooves. An almighty, relentless rhythmic thumping that knocked inside Milena's skull. She called in her sleep, held her pounding head. She heard a door slam shut. But, however hard she strained her eyes, she couldn't see this door, or the gulls or the horses through the thickening fog. She only saw the shape of the crowd in the far distance and the vaporous figure of the girl, gliding further and further away.

Friday 14th January, 1898

The Great Manipulator and the Hovering Hag

All was still in Madam Pinwoman's wagon. Zdenko was fast asleep in the wooden trunk he used as a bed. The snoring seamstress was sprawled on a pile of rags on the floor. Then Zdenka twitched. She opened one eye. Then the other. At precisely the same moment, the first cockcrow of morning rang cross the camp.

Still swathed in the long white sheets she slept in, she eased herself upright and began to unwind the material, one layer at a time. Once free, she slipped out of her hammock and stood over Zdenko.

"I know you're there," he said, both eyes shut tight.

Zdenka pulled hard on each of her fingers, relishing the cracking noise they made.

"And you needn't think that will make me go any faster."

"The Master's expecting us."

Zdenko unbound himself from his sheet, climbed out of his trunk and dressed. He concentrated on tying his shoe laces. He couldn't bear one lace or loop being bigger or longer than the other. Once they were perfectly even he stood, nodded at Zdenka, and they left.

As they marched in tandem through mud and slush across the encampment, Zdenka was glad to see that yesterday's snowfall and frost had been usurped by drizzle and mist. Grey was her favourite colour, and she loved the feel of rain on her face. She looked up at the overcast sky and very nearly smiled. They hastened towards the theatre building and entered through a side door which led directly to a chamber of marionettes, the same cast of characters who had been stored beneath the Master's wagon.

Zdenka immediately ran to Hag Woman. "Spectacular!" she cried, imagining herself older and wiser and just as crooked. "I wish she were mine." As she reached and touched the old crone's hands, its lolling head jerked and nodded towards the door.

"Did you see that?" she squealed, keeping her beady eyes fixed firmly on the marionette. "She moved on her own. Like a real person."

Zdenko marched up to Diablovich and ran his fingers down the ridges of his hoof. "And this feels as if it's come from a real animal."

The Master burst into the chamber. "I'm glad to see you here so early. Our final preparations are in hand."

"We were admiring the marionettes," Zdenko said, peeping from between the dangling legs of the Storyteller.

"Very good, very good. You are beginning to experience the joy to be had from puppets. You are beginning to understand the satisfaction that comes from being a Great Manipulator, or in my case, *the* Great Manipulator. The hand of the puppeteer is the hand of he who leads and, like the parent of an obedient child, he who leads his puppets well will be well rewarded.

"Puppetry is a form of necromancy, a waking of the dead," he continued, striding up and down the rack of marionettes. He paused, his hand on Hag Woman's shoulder. "By itself, the puppet is no more than the materials from which it was made. By itself it is no more than a piece of dead wood. If the puppeteer fails to animate it well, if the audience fails to respond to its actions, there is no show, there is no life."

"Marionettes are there for the manipulating, my malevolent monkeys. They are there to serve, to be sent out into the world to spread the message of he who manipulates them."

"Marionettes are there for the manipulating," Zdenka repeated. "Without the control of a good puppeteer they are no better than the dead. But, Master," she wondered aloud, "is it possible for them to move on their own?"

The Master curled an arm around Zdenka. "Anything is possible, anything. That's what I do, that's who I am, The Puppet Master! My will is their will." He reached and touched Hag Woman's cheek. Her feet shuffled.

Zdenka turned to her brother, one eyebrow raised, wondering if the Master manipulated everyone like this. Even them.

Zdenko responded with a shrug of his shoulder. He wasn't sure. "Master, when will you teach *us* how to make them move without working their strings?"

"Fear not, you both have important roles in my plan. But you must be patient."

"What are these ones called?" asked Zdenka, pointing to two small marionettes seated on a bench at the end of the row.

"Don't touch them! They're not ready . . . their paint isn't dry. I'm moving them back to my wagon later. Now follow me, and I'll show you how you will operate the *pièce de résistance* of the foyer this evening. An enormous marionette representing my esteemed forefather will hang from the centre of the ceiling, and you will control him from a concealed adjoining chamber. I want you to have fun with him. Make his limbs lunge at the audience when they least expect it, sweep his head across the length of the room. Do anything you like, as long as you use him to drive them into a frenzy. Come with me now and I'll introduce you. We have a little time before your next job."

Voice of the Oracle

"I've bought the tickets for the puppet show," called Katerina, closing the door to the House of the Ladies of Snow behind her. "I can't wait to see Milena's face when I show her. Tereza?" Katerina made her way down to the cellar, taking care not to catch her heels in the uneven steps. "Didn't you hear me? I've arranged everything."

"Never mind about that. Milena's in trouble."

"What do you mean? What kind of trouble?" asked Katerina, laying the tickets on the table.

"I don't know exactly, but I've consulted the cards and the stones and they both indicated that danger is near. I'm going to try one last thing." Tereza held up a bunch of fresh hedgemaid.

"Hedgemaid, sometime called ground ivy, or alehoof, has long been valued for its powerful divination properties. Ancient herbalists believed it could also cure insanity and melancholia. It's especially good at revealing who a person's enemy is."

"Oracle, hear my question," Tereza whispered. "Is Milena in any danger?"

She plucked several leaves from the plant and arranged them around the base of a yellow candle. "Watch carefully."

No sooner had she finished speaking, than a chill swept through the cellar, lifting the leaves into the flame. They burned swiftly, transforming into a fine ash that settled on the open pages of Tereza's diary of herbs.

"The leaves only gravitate towards the flame when trouble is brewing."

She tossed a second handful of leaves around the candle. "What is the nature of this danger? Who is the enemy?"

Again they rose but this time, after being drawn into the flame, the leaves hissed and spat sparks across the table.

"The tickets!" Katerina exclaimed, brushing the burning leaves off them. "They're singed."

Tereza extinguished the candle. "I know you're sceptical about this kind of thing, but please, will you trust my intuitions? Will you believe the signs?"

Katerina nodded. It was clear her sister was genuinely distressed. "I'll prepare the horse and carriage. We'll drive to the cottage right away."

Within minutes the Sisters were cantering along Vinohradska Street. They raced down Wenceslas Square, sped across Karluv Bridge. No sooner had they begun the steep descent up Nerudova Hill, Tereza began to shriek.

"Stop, Katerina! Look, there's Baba. Who's she with? Baba! Baba! Wait!"

Baba turned towards the carriage. Her eyes were expressionless, her movements stiff, as if she were made of wood. She raised her hands to her face. It was no longer covered in skin but by a mask. She pulled it off to reveal a second, then a third. Each wooden representation of her real face was more distorted than its predecessor.

Before they had time to climb from the carriage, Baba had been pushed down a side street by the twins and no amount of searching up, down and around Nerudova Hill could locate her. There were no marks in the snow to show where their footsteps had trod.

Filled with terror, Katerina and Tereza went directly to the House of the Golden Acorn.

They banged on the door.

There was no answer.

"Of course, Milena will be at school." Tereza searched through her bag. "Here, take my spare key. You go first."

Katerina opened the door. She walked through the cottage, checked Milena's room. No one was home.

"Come quickly, look at this!" Tereza cried. A note lay on the table.

Dear Baba,

I will be home later than usual
this evening because Lukas an
have been given tickets to see th
marionette show on Petrin Hill.
Can you believe it?! Two of the
Marionette Master's assistants
came and gave them to me late
last night. Tereza and Katerin
going to take us all tomorrow b
these are for the opening night,
and came from the Master.
How could I not go?!

Don't worry, I'll be with
Lukas and I'll come home as soo
as it's finished.

Milena
xx

"You're right," said Katerina. "Something is wrong."

The Show of Shows

"Gather round, my people, gather round!" the Puppet Master ordered. "Before you go to your positions let us take a moment to feast together on our patrons' anticipation. Have you seen the throng waiting at the gates, salivating like hungry dogs? How they will laugh and weep and beg for more! How they will worship the hairs on my chin, the mud on my boots!"

He pushed through the crowd and slapped an arm around Karel.

"Karel, I want you to spend some time among the audience before you begin your work. Head to the front of the theatre, gorge yourself on the atmosphere. You should savour the thrill of your first night, but then check your marionettes. Twins, to your booth. Pinwoman, have your girls wheel the dolls to my wagon then go directly to the wardrobe room. Attendant, to

the gates and make sure you take down the name and address of everyone who enters."

He bowed. "Let the show begin!"

Hundreds of chattering, laughing people had gathered around Petrin Hill. While most of the theatre-goers were from the wealthiest ranks of Prague society, there was also a throng of working folk who had decided it would be well worth spending a week's wages on a ticket. Rich or poor, everyone wore their finest clothes. There were ladies dressed in velvet gowns and fur-trimmed capes and winter bonnets, worried about their new shoes and stockings getting wet and muddy, and there were cooks and seamstresses and typists and stallholders who had powdered their cheeks and dressed up their clothes with brooches and feathers. Gaggles of urchins peeped beneath the fence, desperate to find a gap big enough to squeeze through, while representatives from the city council forced their way to the front of the queue.

To the right of the entrance was a sideshow stand with the words *Mysterious Matka's Den of Dastardly Delights and Perfidious Predictions* embroidered in green and yellow silk on its awning. A voice screeched from behind a curtain.

"Rotten onions will kill your bunions, and unripened cherries will keep you merry," she cackled. "Leave me a coin and I'll clean up your lice. Offer me two for more useful advice!"

The theatre-goers gasped and shrank back against the fence as a boy led a big brown bear along the length of the queue. It roared, reared onto its hind legs. The boy tugged hard on the heavy chains around its neck and ankles. It dropped on all fours.

"La-dies and gen-tle-men, have your tickets ready!" called a man in a jester's costume. "No pushing, tussling, jostling or hustling, please. You're next, young lady. Write your name and address just here. That's it, quick as you like. Now give me a grin and I'll let you in!" The golden bell hanging from the end of his hat tinkled with every jerky nod.

Milena passed the jester her ticket. "May your dreams come true, and your nightmares die an ugly death!" he laughed. "Hurry along, in you go now."

She walked through the gates, her heart thumping with anticipation. Dozens of lanterns glowed through the night mists and, in the distance, beyond the troupes of entertainers and sideshows, Milena saw the theatre building, which looked as grand as any nobleman's home on Old Town Square.

"This was in my dream," said Milena. "It wasn't a marketplace at all. It was a showground."

Before Lukas had a chance to answer, a troupe of drummers led a parade of jugglers, stilt walkers, fire eaters and tumblers past them.

"Fire of fires, thunder divine,
I cast the stones o'er blood red wine!
But what makes me say this silly spell
That summons devils from black Hell?
And what makes me do these silly tricks?
I'll lose my soul if this persists!"

sang a cloaked man bringing up the rear of the procession. He marched to the beat of the drums while a monkey scurried about his ankles.

As they passed, Lukas turned to Milena. "Are you sure this is a good idea?" he asked for the hundredth time. "I mean, if the people who gave you the tickets last night were the ones who attacked us, I think we should go home. It doesn't feel . . . safe."

"Leave if you want, but I'm not going anywhere until I find out what this means. Maybe Karel can help. Do you think we might see him?"

"How should I know? He's probably too busy and important to talk to the likes of us tonight. But if you're determined to stay, I'm not leaving you here alone. We should go to our seats."

They ran the rest of the way to the theatre, past the stand selling baked apples and pancakes, past *Visionary Varushka's Palm Reading Stall*, past the bear now chained to a post, past the pen that proclaimed to contain the *Smallest Man in the Universe*. Breathless, they ground to a halt at the foot of the staircase.

Milena walked through the oak doors.

"What's going on? Lukas? Where are you?" she called. "There doesn't seem to be any way through."

Enclosed in a maze of mirrors, Milena was faced with dozens of distorted reflections of herself, long and thin as a spire one moment, short and squat as a toad the next. Sideways in one mirror, upside down in another. She tried to feel for the edges of the walls, but there were none. Every surface was a mirror. She pushed against the glass with greater force, and to her astonishment one of them swung open to reveal a smaller chamber of mirrors. "It's like being inside a glass onion!"

Milena eventually found her way through and stepped onto the gleaming black floor of the hexagonal art nouveau reception room. Its glass walls were painted with elegant absinthe-green swirls, and the heads of puppets peeped through circles which had been cut into the glass at random points.

"Duck, quickly!" shouted Lukas, as he emerged from the maze after her. He pulled her from the path of a gigantic marionette that had been released from a trapdoor in the foyer's ceiling. The theatre-goers shrieked and clambered to the sides of the room as the marionette soared across the room five, six, seven times before the twins reeled him back inside the hatch.

Milena led Lukas to the auditorium and found their seats in the centre of the front row. As the room fell dark, the men in the audience cheered and stamped their feet, while the ladies waved their handkerchiefs and squealed.

"Why are they making such a racket?" whispered Lukas. "Why is everyone behaving so strangely? Nothing's happened yet."

She pressed a finger to her lips. "Shh! It's about to begin."

"Good evening, Ladies and Gentlemen!" bellowed the Master as he emerged from the curtains at the side of the stage. "Welcome to my Show of Shows! Welcome one and all!" He paused dramatically and flicked out his coat tails.

"Ladies and Gentlemen, I ask you to cast aside all thoughts of this world. Allow yourselves to come to a new understanding of History, Destiny and Truth. A New Age is upon us, and a new life awaits you all." The Master raised both arms, looked up to the glittering ceiling, then stared at the audience. The auditorium fell silent. There was no coughing, rustling, shifting in seats or whispering. There was no more cheering or stamping. The audience sat as stiff as mannequins, barely breathing, frozen like the statues on Karluv Bridge.

Several minutes later the Master stamped his foot.

"La-dies and Gen-tle-men, I give you my 'Legends of the Future'!"

The drone of violins and cellos vibrated through the auditorium as the curtain was raised, revealing a richly painted backdrop of wild meadows and distant forests. The audience let out an involuntary gasp as the stringed instruments reached a glorious, dizzying crescendo and the Story-teller descended from on high.

He made his opening speech and introduced four bearded marionettes.

"Behold the first players in our tale, good people. Here stand Brother Cech, Brother Lech and Brother Rus," his jaw clattered. *"Ambition surges through the veins of each man, but there is none more ambitious, none more driven than the brilliant Brother Bertoldo."*

Cech, Lech and Rus nodded to one another, picked up their walking sticks and clopped away in different directions, leaving the fourth marionette alone, centre stage. He was three heads taller than the others, his beard was longer and thicker, his cheeks redder and more fleshy. He raised his spear, pointed it up to the gods. His teeth jiggled around like stones in a gold-hunter's sifting tray as he opened his mouth and roared from the depths of his belly.

"You are the blood of my blood and your blood is the blood of this land."

Milena shrank back in her seat. The marionette was speaking directly to her.

Sister of Slavic Soil

Katerina and Tereza tiptoed into the auditorium as the curtains fell. They'd had to bribe the Jester to allow them in as the opening night had sold out. They positioned themselves at the back of the hall just as the curtains opened to reveal a stage full of marionettes, all facing the castle that perched on a heap of rocks at the back of the stage.

"Keep your eyes open," Katerina whispered. "Lukas and Milena must be here somewhere."

They struggled to see anyone but those immediately around them; the only light came from the spotlight which illuminated Bertoldo as he stomped onstage in black hunting boots. But it wasn't long before Tereza noticed something was wrong. The audience was completely transfixed. It was if their eyes had been replaced with marbles and their minds emptied of everything except the story that was unfolding before them.

"It's a good thing we missed the start. They've been put into some kind of trance, although our herbs would probably have protected us." Tereza touched the sprig of horehound pinned to her jacket.

Bertoldo pulled an axe from beneath his tunic, clambered up the rocks and opened his fat-lipped mouth.

"Premsyl, I order you to come out of your castle and face the truth. I ask you to explain to me and the people of this fair land what right you have to this Kingdom."

Premsyl emerged from the castle, but before he had a chance to answer Bertoldo's demands, the brute chopped off his head in a single swift blow. It came off cleanly, rolling onto the stage with a thud. Both the audience and huddle of marionettes, who jittered and jangled at the foot of the rocks, cheered uproariously.

Bertoldo raised his hand to silence them as he hobbled to the front of the stage.

"Citizens of Bohemia, I am proud to be your King at last! I have returned to the Kingdom to become your leader and take Libuse as my wife.

"Bow low to welcome Libuse anew as we become man and wife, King and Queen of Bohemia! Vysehrad will rise again and Prague will be mine. No longer Bride of Premsyl, Daughter of Krok or Granddaughter of Cech, but Mistress of the Master! Welcome my Queen of Subservience, your Sister of Slavic Soil!"

Libuse appeared onstage holding her horse by the

reins. A silver crown sat on her ebony hair. She was barefoot and a long gown trailed behind her, a branch of linden hung from her belt. Her features were well-defined, her eyes large and dark, her lips shone like dewy strawberries. She knelt before Bertoldo. He placed a purple cape over her shoulders.

"*Arise my Queen, arise. Accept me as your Lord and Husband. Arise and pledge yourself to me.*"

"This isn't right. This isn't as the story of our people, this isn't the legend." Katerina muttered. "Who on earth is Bertoldo?"

"*Libuse, now that shame is upon your former husband's name and you are mine, your children and powers are also mine and our descendents shall inherit the Kingdom. So it must be forever.*"

The sound of timpani drums reverberated around the auditorium. It built to a thunderous climax as the Storyteller descended.

"Ladies and Gentlemen, our show of shows has come full circle. We have been on a journey through time and have realigned the path of history. The joys of Bertoldo's Kingdom await those who embrace the Master."

The curtain fell and the Puppet Master emerged stage left to euphoric applause. He held out his hands, bowed, then bowed again and again. Still the audience clapped. With a nod and a glare, he silenced them.

"Behold my Star of Stars!"

Libuse joined the Master and curtseyed, somewhat awkwardly.

"Behold my Queen!"

Tereza grabbed Katerina's arm and jumped from her seat. "That isn't a marionette!" she cried. "She's real. It's Ludmila!"

Standing just inside the showground gates, Tereza and Katerina were trying not to get caught up in the swirl of the departing crowd. They had hurried from the auditorium as soon as the final curtain fell, leaving the entranced audience on their feet, applauding as the Master and his marionettes took bow after bow.

"It was her, wasn't it? It really was Ludmila!" said Tereza.

"Yes, it most definitely was Ludmila," Katerina replied.

They clasped hands, scarcely able to believe what they had seen.

"There's Lukas," cried Tereza. "Lukas! Where's Milena?"

Before Lukas could answer he was jostled by a sudden outpouring of theatre-goers surging through the gates, utterly unaware of anything around them. They stared at some unspecified point in the distance, their bodies moved stiffly, no one spoke. The only sound was that of a thousand pairs of shoes treading over grass and mud, then stepping onto the cobblestones.

He eventually fought his way through. "She's gone. One minute we were on our way out, and the next she'd gone. I saw her being dragged through a door in the mirror maze but I couldn't get it open. I tried but it just wouldn't open. She's gone."

A Creak and a Crack and the Scent of Sandalwood

Milena sat up and rubbed her eyes. The room smelled of wood and paint and although she couldn't see them, Milena knew her hands were full of splinters. She touched the back of her aching head. She didn't remember a thing about the performance. She only remembered a pair of grinning identical faces veering towards her from behind the wall of mirrors. She remembered the grip of bony fingers, curling around her throat. She remembered watching herself, as if from above, no longer part of herself, crash to the ground.

Milena groped around the walls, hoping to find a chink in the chamber to force her way through. Her muscles felt like stone, her bones were glass. She couldn't move. "There's no way out!" she gasped.

She heard a creak, and a crack of light shone from the

opposite corner of the room. She heard a match being struck.

The next thing she saw was the Master's face.

"I said we'd meet again soon! We have a big adventure ahead of us. An important adventure," he said, looming closer. "While Cech, Rus and Lech are rolling in their graves, Bertoldo rises from his. One day you will thank me."

"Thank you?" snapped Milena. "Why would I ever have reason to thank you?"

"Come on, stand up! Don't make things difficult for yourself. You have much to look forward to."

The Master went to the chamber door and poked his head into the foyer. "Twins! Where are you? I need some light in here."

Zdenko appeared in the doorway, passed the Master a lamp.

"Have the grounds emptied yet? I can't shift her until they are."

"Yes, Master, the grounds are empty," Zdenka replied. "The audience left like a parade of the living dead."

"Excellent, excellent! You've done an outstanding job this evening. You'll be rewarded for this, my ferocious foxes," the Master promised. "Now go and make sure no one is lurking around my wagon. I'll follow in a few minutes."

He turned to Milena. "I'll give you one last chance to come of your own accord." He held the lamp over her head. "Are you going to stand? Yes? No? Very well,

I shall have to carry you." He covered her with a blanket and flung her over his shoulder like a sack of turnips.

"Why are you doing this to me?" she yelled, kicking him hard in the base of his spine.

"That's not the kind of behaviour I'd expect from the Princess of Prague!" mocked the Master, tightening his grip. "Quite a fighter, aren't you?" he remarked as Milena kicked him again. "But I advise against blowing into the ear of a bear, lest he bite you. Stop your tantrum before I bind your legs, gag your mouth and stick you in the mud like a scarecrow."

Milena fell silent. The Master shifted her weight. He didn't want to resort to using the full force of his special techniques on her. Not yet. She had defended herself well against his hypnotic powers when they first met on the Old Town Square. For the time being, until every piece of his plan was in place, he would control her with old fashioned physical restraint. He walked across the showground and dumped Milena outside his wagon.

She pulled the blanket away from her eyes.

"Come along, in you go!" he said, unlocking the door to his secret chamber. He pulled down the ladder.

Milena grabbed hold of the wheel spokes. "I'm not moving."

The Master honked with amusement as he forced each of her fingers off the wheel and pushed her into the concealed chamber. "Your home is here now." He reached inside his boot for the key, unlocked the cage and, with a flourish, gestured for Milena to go inside.

"Into the cage," he breathed. "I shall visit you tomorrow."

Reluctantly, Milena did as she was told. Everything looked fuzzy through the darkness and dust, as if she was wearing a veil of cobwebs. The sweet aroma of rose and sandalwood filled her nostrils.

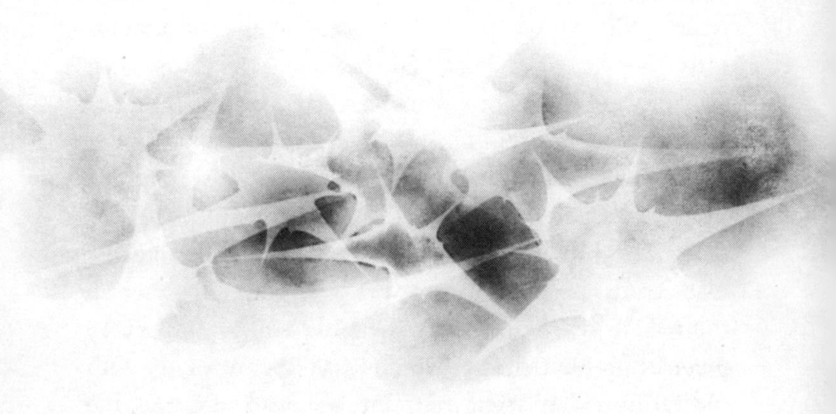

Breaking the Bloodline

Katerina leaned close towards Tereza. Their foreheads touched. "At least we know Ludmila is alive."

"If only I'd consulted my hedgemaid earlier, if only I'd given Milena a better charm, if only I'd . . . "

"Don't blame yourself," Katerina comforted. "It couldn't have been your charms. Lukas is safe. I think I have some inkling as to what might be happening. You noticed what tonight's show was really about – the references to 'seizing power' and 'reclaiming the Kingdom', the way the audience was manipulated as if they, too, were marionettes. Someone is trying to rewrite history, to lay claim over Bohemia."

There was a knock at their front door.

"That will be Lukas and Mr. Laskavy," said Katerina. "Perhaps with news."

Mr Laskavy came into the drawing room. He shook

his head. "I'm sorry. The Chief Inspector was no use. He just stared at us with a peculiar, faraway look. He didn't seem to hear a word we said."

"Everyone I saw in the audience and leaving the showground was the same, Father," said Lukas. "They had the eyes of dead fish."

Mr. Laskavy looked at Katerina and Tereza, then at his son. "Everyone except you three . . . How can that be?"

"I'm a practitioner of herbal medicine. We had charms which protected us," Tereza explained. "Do you still have the horehound I gave you last night, Lukas?"

"Yes, I think so" replied Lukas rummaging in his coat pocket. He was very pale. "It's right here."

"That's why Lukas wasn't affected. It's fortunate you had it with you, Lukas. It builds a kind of fortress around the mind. But it isn't strong enough to ward off physical attack." Tereza pushed back her chair. "We have to get back to the showground and find them before the evil scoundrels pack up and leave town."

Katerina poured Tereza a glass of slivovice. "Sit back down and drink this. It'll calm your nerves. We know he has Ludmila, and Milena too, but I don't think he would hurt them. From what we saw last night they're too important a part of his plan. We've become embroiled in what can only be described as a highly dangerous political and personal conspiracy. We need to find out who this Bertoldo character is. We need to know what he had to do with Cech, Krok and Libuse. We must dissect the legends and end this attempt to break our bloodline."

Maiden, Mother, Crone

Milena moved further into the cage. "Milenka? Milenka? Can it be true?!" Milena stopped dead. Then she walked towards the figure in the shadows. "Maminka? It really is you, isn't it? Everyone said you were dead, but I knew they were wrong, I knew I'd see you again." She flung her arms around her mother's neck.

"Yes, it really is me," Ludmila's voice sounded as warm and soft as honey. She held Milena close. "I'm sorry I've been away from you. How did he lure you here?"

Milena explained how she'd met the Puppet Master on Old Town Square, how she'd been given the mysterious doll that looked just like her and the golden envelope with tickets to the show. She described how the twins had pulled her through the mirror maze; how she'd woken up in the dank room and tried to fight the

Master off. "But none of that matters now we're together. I've been asking you to come home for as long as I can remember. I talk to you every single day."

"I know, Milena, I hear every word, and I hoped you would hear me answer, but the Master . . . "

"What happened? Has he had you all this time?" Milena said. "Is that where you've been?"

"Yes." Ludmila stood. Her gown rippled behind her like a scarlet river. "Yes, I've been held by him since the day your father died.

"Milena, everything's my fault. You know about Libuse? That the women in our family line usually inherit her intuitions, her knowledge of the healing properties of herbs, her visions?"

"I only just found out, but I know."

"And did Baba or your Aunts also tell you I tried to deny Libuse's gift?"

"Yes. Baba said it was too much of a strain."

"It was a strain, but I should have accepted it. Libuse sent me a vision on the morning of that terrible day, but after years of forsaking her, I didn't understand what she was telling me. It was too indistinct, too patchy. Like trying to fit together pieces from different jigsaw puzzles. But as I slept after lunch that afternoon, the pieces fell into place. I saw that he was in great danger. About to be murdered. I knew I had to go to the theatre as soon as possible."

"Murdered? I thought it was an accident, that he had fallen . . . Wait . . . I've seen it in my dreams . . . I . . . I saw someone grab him. That's how he died, isn't it? He was pushed."

"Yes Milena, that's how he died." Ludmila nodded, closing her eyes. "Then the Master and the twins came for me. For weeks I had no idea where we were bound. I didn't see a soul. Once a day the wagon stopped and someone brought me food but they were always masked, or wearing hooded cloaks. The wagon trundled on and on for what seemed like an eternity. I could tell we were travelling far from Prague, that we were crossing the country on rough tracks. I didn't dare ask Libuse for help after I had turned my back on her. I supposed she had forsaken me for good, and who could blame her?

"We eventually stopped on the outskirts of a village and only then did I see my captor, the Master. I remember thinking that I recognised him. I presumed he was a jealous rival puppet master, but over time I learned the truth. Over time I began to understand why I'd been taken. And the more I discovered, the more I worried for your safety, for I knew the Master planned to return for you once any suspicion aroused by your father's death had subsided."

"But what does he want with us? Why did he take you?"

Ludmila began to pace around the cage. "He's a madman, deranged. He believes his family suffered in the days when Cech settled his people in Bohemia, when Rus ruled Russia, when Lech was King of

Poland. He believes that his ancestor, a man the Master calls Brother Bertoldo, should have been crowned King of Bohemia. Bertoldo tried to usurp Krok but his attempts to seize power were overthrown and he was outlawed. He was left in the thick of the woods in the middle of winter and was never seen again. The Master has set himself the task of avenging Bertoldo. That's why I was captured, why he forced me to be his puppet, why he made me play the part of Libuse. He's dedicated his whole life to tracking us down, to perfecting the art of mind manipulation, of hypnotism. And while I've fended off falling completely under his control, at times I've been helpless."

"Why would kidnapping us help him?" asked Milena.

"Through controlling me, he believes he is sharing in Libuse's powers, as Premsyl did. I've been forced to learn his scripts, to act out his distorted version of history. He thinks he can use our blood links to Libuse and Krok and Cech to legitimise his ambitions. He believes that by making us his family he can steal our heritage, claim the powers of Krok's three daughters for himself, and so fulfil his ancestor's quest to be crowned King of Bohemia.

"He realised that in order to do this he needed to have complete control on a grander scale. Unless we find a way to stop the show, the Master will soon have control over the whole city. He's already ruined the lives of so many people, so many children." Ludmila lowered her head.

"What do you mean? What others?"

Ludmila reached through the side of the cage and gently nudged a bundle of rags. Two figures uncurled themselves.

"Do you recognise them? It's Ruzena and Pavel. They won't know who you are." Ludmila waved a hand across their faces. "See, no response. They can't blink anymore. They don't speak. And there are others. I hardly know which puppets might once have been humans."

As Milena tried to take in the horror her mother had revealed, a cough came from the far corner of the chamber.

"Who's there?" called Ludmila.

"Maybe it's Lukas. He's bound to be looking for me."

"Milena?" came Baba's frail voice. "Ludmila?"

The door to the chamber slammed open.

The Rotten Apple

"W-w-what are you doing here?" Karel stammered as he saw the Master's prisoners. Bedraggled, covered in sawdust, they looked as if they belonged in an asylum or, at the very least, quarantined in an infirmary. "What's going on?"

Ludmila walked towards him, strings still attached to her arms and neck, face stained with tears only a real human could produce. "Listen to me, Karel. I'm not a puppet. Look, no one's pulling my strings. I'm the Master's prisoner. He forced me to be his marionette. He's distorted your memories, twisted your mind. He has control over all of us, he's using us to realise his crazed ambitions. Everyone who sees the show will fall prey to his power in the same way."

"Keep away from me," said Karel as he withdrew from the cage. He'd spent the evening admiring how

uncannily lifelike the Libuse marionette had seemed, but the thought that she might be a real person had never crossed his mind. "Don't talk about the Master like that. He's been like a father to me."

"Do good for the Devil and he'll reward you with evil," Baba warned. "Release us and we will rescue you a thousand times over."

"You're lying. I don't need rescuing from someone who gave me a new life."

"Do you want to live in the clutches of the Master forever?" Ludmila said, extending her arm through the bars of the cage. As her fingers touched the back of his neck a chill charged through his body, tingling down his spine and into his fingers and toes. For a moment he saw his father's farm.

"You have to believe us, Karel," said Milena, her face flushing. "You'll help, won't you?"

Their eyes locked. A second chill rushed through him.

"Milena?" he said, brushing his hair from his face. "Why are you in my Master's wagon? You shouldn't be here."

"And neither should they," she replied, pointing to Pavel and Ruzena. "They're not marionettes either. None of us should be here. You have to help us."

Karel felt sick. "Was it my Master? Did he lock you up too?" he asked, barely able to get the words out.

Milena nodded. "Do you know where he keeps the key?"

"No, but I could try . . ."

"Then leave now," Milena interrupted, "find my aunts, tell them where we are. They live in the house at the end of Vinohradska Street, near the National Museum. And find Lukas too; you know the boy from the shop. Please, do something, Karel. Hurry!" she cried, shaking the cage.

A bell sounded above them.

"Look, there he is, the rotten apple. Just as we said. We knew he was up to no good," spat Zdenko.

"Yes, we knew he was doing something wrong. He's nothing but a stupid, slimy traitor," hissed Zdenka.

The Master pushed past the twins and clambered inside. "How dare you betray me!" he yelled, grabbing Karel's wrists. "After all I've given you, all I've done for you. You are going to suffer like a slaughtered pig. How did you find this place?"

"I saw you here, Master, that night. I . . ." Karel faltered. "I only wanted to see if this was where you keep the main marionette. I thought I should know. The twins do."

The Master threw Karel through the hatch, jumping down after him and kicking him as he lay cowering. Blood seeped from a wound on his head. The Master watched it drop like a cherry into a patch of virgin snow.

"Zdenko! Zdenka! Follow me. This treacherous snake belongs behind the mirror maze."

Karel opened his eyes. He kicked against the wall in frustration when he realised he was imprisoned. A thousand thoughts raced through his mind. Why hadn't he insisted on seeing the Libuse marionette before the show? Why hadn't he acted more quickly when he discovered the cage?

In the time since Libuse had laid her fingers on him, memories had begun to return in blinding flashes; waking up in the bedroom he shared with his brothers, breakfasting on the newly laid eggs his sister had collected from her chicken pen, spending the morning running in the fields with his dog.

Karel touched the wound on his head. No father would do this to his son. He felt shame. He felt guilt. He would put right these wrongs the moment he escaped. He would rescue Milena if it was the last thing he did.

A Doll for Every Door

The city of Prague in the dead of night was usually a place of peaceful desertion. The river might run hard and fast and crash little waves onto the rocks of the riverbank, the ducks might quack and flap their wings through the water, or the rain might lash, but the city's nighttime wanderers were quiet, calm kinds of creatures. They wandered to walk away their worries, to experience the city in solitude. They meandered along the riverbank, leaned over railings, touched the soil in the parks, the bark of the trees, the stones on the ground.

But tonight the streets were not for those seeking solitude. Tonight they streamed with those who had experienced *Legends of the Future*. They were flooded with people who had transformed Prague into a city of ghosts. They walked through the night-mists like phantoms. They roamed streets and alleyways, lanes and arcades with nothing but thoughts of the Master. And so it was all across the city.

Once the Jester had shooed the last of the lingering urchins from the gates, the Master's marionettes began to appear around the showground. Each danced to their own rhythm as, manipulated by the Master, they made their way to the box office. There was the Jester, somersaulting wildly. There Lady of Barley, plucking feathers from her pocket and offering them to the Story-teller. Hag Woman pulled on her jutting jaw, twirled on her gnarled legs like a spinning top. And there was Diablovich, chasing his tail, gnashing his teeth.

Zdenka gasped when she saw them. Her heart fluttered like the wings of a newborn bird.

"Have you seen how many dolls we have to deliver?" she said, glancing back at the carts they were dragging behind them. "And each of the marionettes has a barrowful too."

She picked up one of the dolls their mother and her seamstresses had worked tirelessly to complete. Each was fashioned in the image of its intended recipient, glass eyes shining like polished gemstones. "Do you think it's really possible for us to get everything done before dawn?

Zdenko didn't reply. A curious smile spread across his face. He lowered his eyes and began to speak in a voice that sounded uncannily like the Master's. "By itself, the puppet is no more than the materials from which it was made. By itself it is no more than a dead thing. Marionettes are there for the manipulating. They are there to serve, to be sent out into the world to spread the message of he who manipulates them."

Zdenka pulled on her plaits. "Aren't you going to answer me?"

"We're his chosen ones. We won't disappoint him, but *we* will control them. The Master's not the only one they obey. We have the power too."

Zdenko clapped his hands. "Take hold of your carts and do as we do," he ordered.

The marionettes followed their young leaders across Karmelitska Street, the wheels of their barrows squeaking like nails down a blackboard as they crossed the cobblestones and tram lines.

"The time has come," breathed Zdenka, tilting her head towards the heavens.

When the procession reached the corner of Prokopska and the Maltese Square, Zdenko gave his sister a list of names and addresses.

"We have to make sure we visit the city's dignitaries and councillors first. Leave a doll on the doorstep of every address on the list, and leave a leaflet for the show for everyone else. Can you do it?"

"Of course I can," said Zdenka. She couldn't bear it when Zdenko tried to take the upper hand. She clicked her fingers and ushered the marionettes south, leaving a doll on the doorstep of everyone who had seen the show, then marking off each house on her list, as the Master had instructed.

"Now it's your turn," she called, sending the marionettes off in different directions. "Off you go!" she called as Hag Woman lurched down Nosticova.

The marionette turned and grinned at Zdenka before laying down a doll.

When the twins returned to the Maltese Square shortly before dawn they knew exactly who was under the Master's control and exactly who had yet to see the show.

Overnight news of the Master's greatness spread across the city as fast as fire through a drought stricken forest, so much so, that the members of the Grand Council of Prague were not at all surprised to be summoned from their beds. By the time the sun rose, they had gathered outside their chambers beneath the Astronomical Clock on Old Town Square, dressed in the ceremonial robes reserved for only the most important state occasions, each clutching an effigy of themselves. Not even the sight of a pair of crimson uniformed marionettes standing guard either side of the doors elicited as much as a raised eyebrow.

The clock struck six and the twelve men filed inside. By the time the figure of Death had jerked his way across the clockface, they were all seated in the principal meeting room.

The Head of the Grand Council picked up a small wooden hammer and knocked on the table.

"Gentlemen, I would not have called you here at this hour unless it was a matter of supreme importance."

The men nodded in agreement.

"The matter to which I refer is the future of our city, which I have led for almost eight years. However, I have decided to relinquish my position as Head of the Grand Council for the good of our great city." He paused, staring into the distance. "A far better leader walks among us. I bow to his superiority. All who agree, stand now."

All twelve councillors pushed back their chairs and stood.

"Then, the time has come."

ACT FOUR
Saturday 15th January, 1898

Smetana's Sign and the War of the Women

The people of Prague woke to find their city ravaged by one of the cruellest winter nights it had ever experienced. The waters of the Vltava had frozen solid, the streets were encased in thick sheets of black ice. No one could remember such coldness, such bitterly unforgiving winds.

Katerina and Tereza had worked through the night, unaware of the severe conditions outside. Katerina had barricaded herself in the drawing room and tried to find out more about Brother Bertoldo but, after failing to come across a single mention of him in any of her books, she had turned to her volumes on human nature in the hope of understanding the Puppet Master's motivation, and the methods of hypnosis he was using.

She read how the priests and priestesses of Ancient Hebrew and Egyptian civilisations had put themselves into trances through incantation and breathing

techniques, but while that was fascinating enough, Katerina was more interested in the scientific basis of hypnosis. She finally found what she was looking for in a journal of psychiatry.

JOURNAL OF PSYCHIATRY

The Theories of Jean-Martin Charcot, 1825-1893.

Charcot was arguably the first great European theorist of hypnosis. After studying the behaviour of his patients in a Parisian clinic which specialised in treating hysteria, he concluded that the hypnotised state was very similar to an attack of hysteria. He also believed that only those afflicted by hysteria could be fully hypnotised.

Charcot observed three distinct stages to the process by which hysterics succumb to hypnosis –

1. **Rigidity**, including stiff limbs that remain in same position when moved and loss of muscle control.

2. **Lethargy** i.e. a state of extreme tiredness.

3. **Sleepwalking**, a disorder characterised by the sleeping sufferer engaging in activities normally associated with wakefulness. The victims' eyes may have an empty appearance and, if questioned, the subject will be unable to respond intelligibly.

She felt she was finally beginning to understand how the Master and his show were having such an effect.

"Let me see . . . " she said, thinking out loud. "His persistent claim that his is the greatest show in the world made everyone in the city desperate to see it. Stirred into a frenzy, his audience is susceptible to the hypnotic techniques he uses during the performance."

"And now they're sleepwalking through the streets, still under his control. What a brilliant piece of psychological theatre. Only a madman could do this." She continued to read.

Tereza was working in the cellar, herbs and potions and scribbled notes cluttering every inch of her work table.

"What shall I do now, Tereza?" asked Lukas, desperate to be involved in all efforts to bring Milena home. He was in an agony of guilt. He still believed he was responsible for her capture. "I've finished sealing the doors and windows with Devil's Apple."

"Good work, thank you. If you're happy to continue helping, would you mind checking that cupboard for my Dictionary of Herbs? It has to be here somewhere."

"Of course," he replied, "although there don't seem to be any books, just stacks and stacks of magazines."

"Let me see that!" exclaimed Tereza, pouncing on the theatre programme Lukas had begun to flick through.

"It's Vlasta and Sarka! A sign from Libuse." Tereza hurried up the cellar steps.

"Lukas has found a way, we have the answer! Do you remember, Katerina? When Ludmila went missing my first thought was that she had gone to Sarka's forest."

"Lukas, you're a genius!" Tereza beamed. "As soon as you showed me this drawing, I realised what we need to do. It's all laid out for us in the tale of Sarka and Vlasta, those exceptional women who fought for freedom in Libuse's name back in Premsyl's time."

Chapter Two

Wild Sarka

"Following Libuse's death, her husband founded the Premyslid dynasty and from that day forth only his sons and their sons and their sons could lead the people of Bohemia. Women were excluded from public life. The Daughters of Bohemia were destined to be silent supporters of their fathers or husbands.

"Furious at this cruel turn of events, bands of women rose up against the men. Many left their husbands and homes and plotted revenge. Just as the men had mocked the women for being long of hair but short of sense, so the women mocked the men's mead-soaked beards. They were led by Vlasta to a hill opposite Vysehrad, on the left bank of the Vltava. There they built a castle called Devin and spent their days hunting and shooting with arrows fashioned by their own hands.

"Premsyl saw Vlasta's castle being constructed, watched her women prepare for war. He called a meeting of his elders. 'Good men, I have assembled you to issue a warning. You have all seen how the

women are arming themselves for battle, how they have built themselves a castle?'

"The elders laughed. 'We have, Lord, but women are weak compared with the might of men. We have nothing to fear.'

"Premsyl chastised them. 'You are fools to speak so. Last night I dreamed of a maiden who stormed through our land like a mad creature. Her hair was wild, her face distorted by fury. In her presence the clear water of our streams turned to blood. The woman drank it like a rabid wolf and forced me to drink also. This is a sign, good men, a sign that we should prepare to defend ourselves from the wrath of women who feel they have been wronged. This is a sign that the power of the women has worked its way into the very heart of our land. It runs through the rivers, sprouts in the forests, and so it will always be, for Libuse has spoken.'

"The elders did not heed their King's warning. They continued to go about their business while Vlasta continued to prepare her women for battle. The tallest were trained to guard Devin Castle. The most beautiful were trained to lure the men. The most agile and athletic were archers. These women worked from Devin, where there was not a man to be found, while others remained among the men at Vysehrad and worked as Vlasta's spies. They stole spears and arrows and horses for her and soon the men were left with no means of defence. The men finally decided to act. They thought it would be enough for them to advance on Devin Castle, that they would have no need of weapons, that feminine fear would force the women to abandon their mission.

"The men approached the castle and saw no sign of Vlasta or her followers. 'You see,' said one, 'they've all fled.' But he didn't notice the women's eyes peering through the slits in Devin's rampart. He didn't hear the women draw their weapons. No sooner had he finished speaking than arrows began to rain down upon them. The gates of Devin opened and, led by Vlasta, hundreds of women on horseback charged at the men. She killed several of the strongest with a single stab of her spear, and her archers struck down dozens of Premsyl's warriors.

"Battered and humiliated, the men left standing hurried back to Vysehrad. News of Vlasta's success spread fast and many more women hastened to Devin. Those who remained with the men were greatly feared by their husbands, who fled to the forests lest they be attacked by their wives as they slept.

"Slowly the men began to re-arm themselves, but Premsyl forbade them to have contact with any woman while they strengthened themselves. Most of the men heeded the King's counsel but Ctirad, one of Vysehrad's strongest and most headstrong soldiers, ignored him.

"While Ctirad was walking though the wooded land that came to be known as Divoka Sarka Forest, he and his men stumbled upon a beautiful young woman seated on a tree trunk. Her wrists and ankles were bound with twine, a jar of mead stood next to her, a hunting horn hung around her neck. When she saw the men approach Sarka began to cry.

"'Good Sirs, I beg you, come to my aid! My father and I were out hunting when I lost my way following a stag. Just when I thought I'd found my path, a band of girls from Devin sprang from the undergrowth and made fun of me for staying with my old father. They tied me up, drank from this jar of mead and began to laugh and dance as if possessed by demons. Please, help me.' Sarka implored.

"Ctirad found it impossible to resist the girl's charms, for she was Vlasta's most beautiful disciple. He untied her, then picked up the jar of mead and sniffed it, curious as to how it could have made the women so merry. He and his men took a swig. It tasted unlike anything they had ever drunk. They guzzled down more and more sweet mead, but as soon as they emptied the jar they began to feel very weak and sleepy. Sarka wasted no time in blowing her hunting horn. A gang of women jumped from the bushes and killed Ctirad's men. They tied him up and brought him to Devin, where he was fixed to a large wheel outside the women's castle so all the men could see him being tortured. And from that day hence, no sane man has dared venture to this forest alone, lest they be tricked and struck down by the spirit of Sarka and Vlasta's women.'

"That, my friends, is the Legend of Divoka Sarka, the Story of the Women's War," Tereza concluded. "It is said that the forest is still charged with the strength of Vlasta and her followers. Just as they triumphed, so Katerina and I will rescue our women from the clutches of the Master."

Katerina pursed her lips and tapped a finger on her cheek as she thought everything through. "We need to find a way to coax the Master to the forest. We can be sure that where he goes, Milena, Ludmila and Baba will go too. A man with his ego wouldn't trust anyone else with looking after them."

She picked up a pen and a sheet of writing paper.

"We'll use this to draw the Master to Divoka Sarka. If he believes it's genuine, he'll come despite the legend. Lukas, would you mind delivering this to the showground right away? Tereza will arm you with her most powerful protections. But before you go, may I borrow one of your flutes? I need one with a shrill, sharp tone, if possible."

"Of course. I have just the thing."

"Once you've delivered the letter, wait for us here.

We must remain as close to Sarka's story as possible, which means Tereza and I must do this alone."

The morning sun rose, high enough to send a ray of light into the room and across Katerina's face. She looked at Tereza and smiled. "For we are the army of women."

THE GRAND COUNCIL OF PRAGUE

Town Hall
Old Town Square
Old Town Prague

15th January 1898

Honourable Sir,

In recognition of your services to the advancement of Bohemian culture, the Councillors of the City and I wish to invite you to an official Ceremony of State to inaugurate you as Ruler of the City of Prague.

The ceremony will be held at noon today in Divoka Sarka Forest, as is the tradition. We look forward to presenting you with your robes and chains of office, and the keys to the city, on this momentous historical occasion.

Yours obediently,
Head of the Grand Council of Prague

Born of Bertoldo

"Something's been left for you," said Zdenko, handing the Master the sealed envelope that had been pushed beneath the wagon door.

The Master tore it open. "Excellent! I'm to be inaugurated as Ruler of the City. Look at this. I've been offered the keys to the city! And the ceremony is to take place at a place of national importance. How exquisitely ironic; they have failed to realise I already have control of them. Apart from the foul and unexpected incident of Karel's betrayal things are progressing as planned. But, it is essential we keep spreading the message. Any lapse will weaken my hold."

Zdenka sidled closer to the Master. "Do you need us to do anything else this morning? We've already positioned fifty more marionettes around the city. They're guarding the Castle gates, the Lesser Quarter Bridge Tower, Karluv Bridge and Wenceslas Square as

well as the Old Town Square."

"Excellent work, but yes, there is one thing," mused the Master. "I want the girl to be introduced to future performances. When we return from our excursion I want her to learn the act I have added to the script. She is to appear as the Daughter of Bohemia, the child of Bertoldo and Libuse. You can be responsible for making sure she learns her new lines."

Zdenka rolled her eyes. This told Zdenko that she didn't want to do anything to help that stupid girl. He twitched his agreement.

The Master stood and pulled on his overcoat. "Once I'm firmly established in Prague, we shall travel west to Karlovy Vary. Then east to the Giant Mountains of Krkonose. My message must spread far and wide. We'll perform four times a day in each town we visit. And by the time the first snowdrops peep their little heads through the earth, I shall return to Prague to be crowned King of Bohemia and Ludmila will become my wife. With the reincarnation of Libuse beside me, and Bertoldo's fire in my blood, the world will beg to be ruled by me.

"But for now, we're going to Divoka Sarka Forest. I'm going to lock our guests up here while we travel. They could do with an airing, especially Ludmila. Her performance last night was less than perfect. She looked tired, distracted even. Perhaps a change of scenery will refresh her."

The Master ushered Milena, Ludmila and Baba out

of the cage and into his living quarters. "I haven't time to feed you this morning. We're going on a journey. I'm about to be given the keys to the city. I suppose I should thank you for allowing me to drain you of your ancestral charms, what do you say, my lovely Queen?"

"Things have progressed more rapidly than I'd anticipated," Ludmila sighed as the Master bolted the door behind them.

"I wonder what's happened to Karel," said Milena, her voice quivering. "And Lukas." She sank into the Master's armchair. "Why haven't they come for me? What will we do if they never come?"

"Quiet in there!" the Master called. "Take the reins, Zdenko."

When the Birds Have Flown

Clouds were gathering over Divoka Sarka Forest. They made the sky heavy and grey, pushed it closer to the earth. A waterfall crashed and careered down a rocky precipice. Even the towering trees bowed to the winds that rushed between their branches.

As soon as she saw the Master's wagon, Katerina pulled a veil over her face and picked up the jar containing the muddy green infusion Tereza had prepared for the Master's consumption.

"We're here, Master. Look, the Council has sent someone to welcome you," said Zdenko. The twins pulled the horses to a standstill.

"On behalf of the Grand Council of Prague, I thank you for coming," Katerina curtseyed. "You must be in need of refreshment after your journey. Please, drink this warming brew before I lead you to the Men

of the Council."

The Master stepped onto the rocky ground and took the jar from Katerina. He sipped a little, smacked his lips together.

"We call it 'Crown for a King'. Please, drink!" Katerina smiled. In order for the mixture of wormwood and crushed belladonna berries to have the desired effect, it was essential that the Master drank at least half of it.

He guzzled down mouthful after mouthful. "Where exactly are they waiting for me? And where are my robes? I was promised new robes."

"It's not far," Katerina assured him. "Your robes and chains of office are there. Goodness! Where did you two spring from? I've never seen such indistinguishable twin brothers and sisters."

"First we were there," replied Zdenka, tilting her head towards the driver's seat.

"And then we were there," added Zdenko, gesturing to the underside of the wagon with a swish of his cloak.

"And now we're here," Zdenka concluded. "May I have a drink too?" she asked.

"It's not suitable," said Katerina.

"Nonsense," interrupted the Master. "I know what's good for them."

Zdenka drank the last of the brew, screwing up her face as each burning drop trickled down her throat.

"Lead on. I can't be away from the showground for long."

As they headed out of sight of the wagon towards the

waterfall, Katerina noticed the Master was already unable to walk in a straight line. She pulled Lukas' flute from her pocket and blew as hard as she could. "That will let them know we're on our way."

"What was that?" asked Baba.

Inside the wagon, with an ear pressed to the wall, Milena gasped. "It sounded like one of Lukas' flutes. He's come for me!"

"We have to find a way to open this door." Ludmila's eyes darted around the room.

"What about this?" asked Milena pulling a sword from a box of props.

"That could do it." Ludmila started trying to prise the door open.

Outside a cloud burst with an almighty explosion of thunder. A bolt of lightning struck a tree trunk. Then, as if a shadow had fallen across the sun, a pair of screeching gulls alighted on the wagon. Then came another pair. Then a dozen more. Soon the ground around the Master was transformed into a sea of birds. A second bolt of lightning cracked at his feet. It felled him like a great oak. Zdenko waded through the birds to the Master's aid.

"Quick!" called Ludmila, reaching outside to unfasten the bottom half of the door. "Milena, I'll help

Baba and you follow. Run from the wagon as fast as you can." Ludmila kissed her daughter before linking arms with Baba and guiding her out of the wagon.

Zdenka saw the door open, but as she moved towards the wagon she collapsed.

"What should I do? They're escaping!" Zdenko panicked.

"Go after them, go after them," the Master ordered as he tried to heave himself onto his elbows. His breathing was short, his voice shaky. Salty sweat dripped from his forehead. "She cannot be allowed to go free. I'll lose control of everything I've worked for. I'll be ruined."

The ground before him merged into a swirling mass of white. He strained to distinguish the indistinct shapes he saw through the lashing rain and shrieking birds.

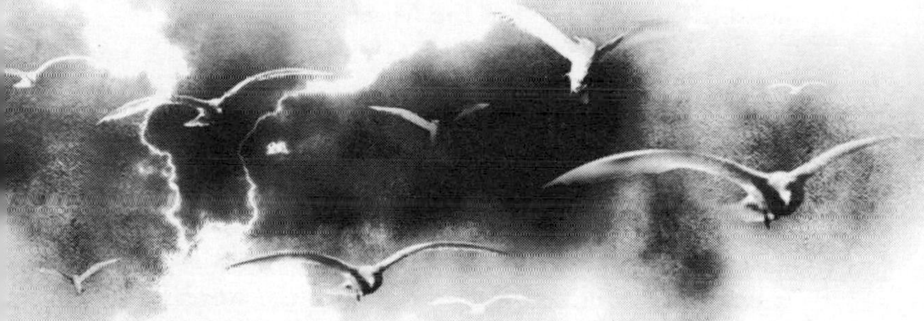

He didn't see Ludmila and Baba running from the wagon. Instead, to his horror, he saw dozens of black-trunked trees ripping their great, gnarled roots from the ground. He saw them lumber towards him. He watched their branches claw the air, felt the quake of their encroachment.

"No! Leave me alone" he shouted, covering his ears and eyes. "Get them away from me! Do something, before they trample me to death, or eat me alive!"

Zdenka was standing in the doorway as the Master rolled onto his side, cursing the world and everything in it. A sudden flurry of wind slammed the door into her, knocking her backwards. She fell, awkwardly twisting her knee. She couldn't move.

For the very first time, Zdenko disobeyed the Master. Rather than pursue Ludmila and Baba, he went directly to Zdenka.

"Are you hurt?" he asked. She didn't answer. He leaned close to her chest and listened hard. She was breathing, but her usually stiff body had become strangely limp. He lifted her and carried her back to the wagon, then returned to the Master.

"The trees . . . I saw them. As clearly as I can see my own hand. Take me back to my camp." His voice trailed to a faint whisper. "I feel as though I'm dying . . . as if every vessel in my body is about to burst."

"I'll drive us home," said Zdenko, savoring the fact that the Master was at his mercy. He lashed the reins and a swarm of birds fled from the roof of the wagon.

Ludmila ran to greet her sisters. "I knew you would come for us. I knew Libuse would send you."

Neither Tereza nor Katerina answered.

"What is it? Where's Milena?"

Katerina shook her head.

"But she was right behind us. Libuse, haven't I been punished enough already?" she screamed into the storm. "Milena!"

The last of the gulls swooped through the trees as the wagon vanished among them. The world fell silent.

Severing of the Strings

The storm shifted. It stalked the Master as he journeyed from Divoka Sarka Forest to Petrin Hill. It raged through villages and hamlets on the outskirts of Prague, ravaging fences and barns, tearing tiles from roofs, terrifying livestock. Zdenko struggled to control the horses. They faltered through water-logged lanes, battled roads blocked by fallen trees. But nothing could have prepared him for what they faced in the heart of the city.

The ice covering the Vltava had begun to melt and its waters were rising fast. The riverbank had burst, deluging houses, transforming Karluv Bridge and the gardens and parks into a floodland.

"Look!" cried Zdenko as he steered the wagon towards Petrin Hill. He shook Zdenka. She sat bolt upright, fully recovered, as if she had just enjoyed an afternoon nap. "What's going on?" she asked. "It looks like something from a nightmare, only we're awake."

The showground was in chaos. The gate and fences had been torn down; the box office overturned. Pieces of scenery, props and costumes were being washed away by the swelling waters. The mirror maze was a mountain of broken glass.

Zdenka looked around the camp. "I wonder where Mother is?" she said, twirling her plaits. "But, more importantly, what's happened to the marionettes?" She sloshed through the muddy water to the puppets piled around a tree. She clapped. Nothing happened. She clicked her fingers. Still nothing happened. They remained lifeless. "They're as good as dead," she said. "We should gather as many as we can, we can't leave them here."

Zdenko grabbed Diablovich's arms while Zdenka untangled Hag Woman, who was dangling by her strings from a low branch. They dragged the puppets to the wagon. Zdenko opened the door.

"Where's my mother? Where have you taken them?" asked Milena.

"They've gone," said Zdenko, "and you'll never see them again."

"How would you know?" Milena yelled, forcing herself to her feet. "They'll come for me soon."

"No, you don't," said Zdenka, knocking Milena backwards with a flick of her wrist. "Forget about her, Zdenko. You see if the Master's any better. I'll take the marionettes inside."

Zdenko returned to the driver's seat and shook the

Master awake. He spluttered, his brain still swirling with the lingering effects of Tereza's brew. Then he saw his beloved theatre. He looked from Zdenko to Zdenka, from Zdenka to Zdenko. "What's happen . . .?" He let out an almighty howl. "There was never going to be an inaugural ceremony, was there? I've been tricked by a woman for a jug of poisoned absinthe and the promise of robes. I've been no better than a village idiot."

"I'm sorry to tell you," said Zdenka, "but you really should know. Libuse and the old woman escaped."

"What? They escaped?"

"Yes, but we haven't lost all of them, we still have the girl," said Zdenko, hastening to pacify the Master. "She's exactly where you left her."

"Is that so, my devils of duality? Then I may still be saved. Ludmila will waste no time in coming for her daughter. The girl is the perfect bait. Be warned; she will come in the spirit of Libuse. She will invoke the conquering spirit of Cech and Krok. She will try to destroy me. A battle awaits us, my friends. Do you think you are strong enough?"

"Yes, Master," replied the twins in unison.

"Of course you are," he said. "Tomorrow I shall proceed as planned with the establishment of my Kingdom. There'll be seats for you at the side of my throne. If, however, you fail me, I'll leave you to rot. Do you hear me? Weakness and failure have no place in my Kingdom.

"To Vysehrad!" he rasped.

Man of Feathers, Man of Fur

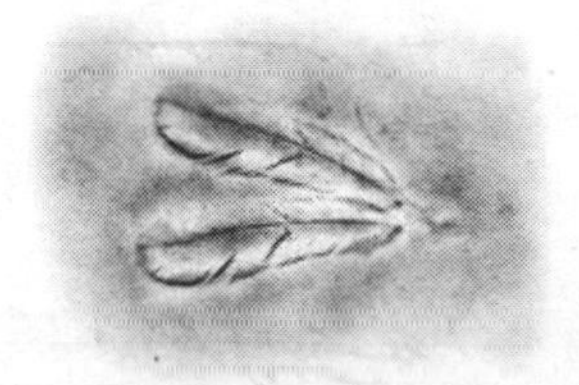

Karel pulled himself from the wreckage of the mirror maze, his face covered in cuts. He left the encampment and turned onto Karmelitska Street. He was hungry and felt more lonely than he had thought possible. In the aftermath of the storm, Prague was a city that had been abandoned even by its ghosts.

Karel couldn't stop walking. He worried that if he stayed still for too long his bones would freeze and crack and crumble to a pile of white dust. He worried that he would fall asleep on his feet and never wake up. He followed the curl of the Brook of the Little Devil southwards. It reminded him of the river that snaked through his village. He wondered if they ever thought of him there. Karel had always imagined the day of his homecoming would be a glorious event; he'd always expected to return a celebrated and prosperous puppeteer. That wasn't going to happen now.

He turned up the collar of his coat, strode across Legionnaire's Bridge, paused outside the National Theatre. A grimy watermark sullied the grand façade but its crown of black and gold and the turquoise stallions rearing on the balustrade were still defiantly handsome.

"Hey, boy!" called a gravelly voice. "Come here, see what I have for you."

Karel turned and saw a dishevelled figure near the theatre door.

"Would you like to see my birds?" grinned the toymaker. "Look at him go! Cheep, cheep little bird! Observe how he flaps his wings and pecks my palm! Would you like to take this fine fellow home with you? Or perhaps this one; or this one, or this one," he said shaking his necklace of furry mechanical mice. "I have plenty for you to choose from. Look, every colour, every size, and every type you could possibly wish for. Which would you like? A crown a piece."

"I don't see any birds," Karel replied, "and I don't have any money but you're welcome to have this crust."

Karel sat next to the toymaker and passed him the bread. "Do you know Prague well? Do you know where Vinohradska Street is?"

"Perhaps. Do you have anything else to eat?"

Karel turned out his pockets. "That's all I had. I've only been in the city a few days and I don't know my way around but I have to find this place. I think it's near the National Museum. Some people have been kidnapped, one of them a young girl. I have to find her family."

"What girl?" asked the toymaker. "Why's she been kidnapped?"

"She's called Milena."

"Milena, you say? Walk east until you reach Wenceslas Square. Then head south until you reach the museum. Vinohradska Street is behind it, to the left."

"Thank you!" replied Karel. "Thank you."

"If you find who you're looking for, be careful," the toymaker warned, waggling a finger in the air. A shower of feathers fell from his sleeve.

Karel looked at the blackened statues of Karluv Bridge, desperate to find the house before nightfall.

Stirring in the Soil

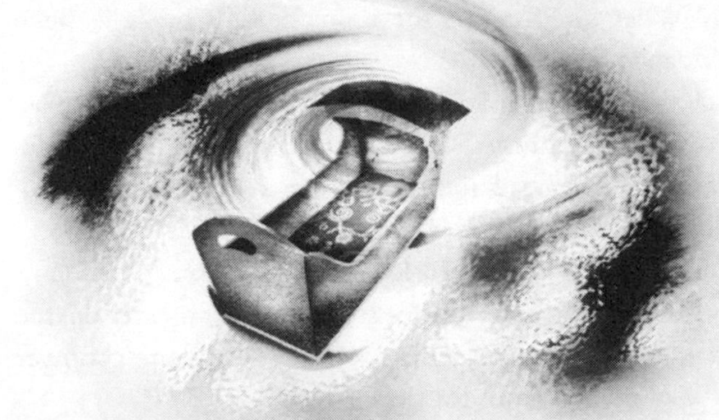

Ludmila lingered in the forest long after the last drops of rain had fallen. She'd sent Katerina and Tereza home and stood at the edge of the waterfall, staring into the frothing abyss until darkness came.

Then she walked until she reached a clearing strewn with pine needles. The hollow hoot of an owl rang through the woods. Ludmila looked up and, through the towering firs, she saw an indigo sky and dozens of flickering stars. She closed her eyes and thought of Libuse.

When she opened her eyes she saw a pool of water. She plunged both hands through the pool's flat surface and drank with a furious thirst. As the water slipped down her throat, she saw a place where three rivers met. She saw a great mountain overlooking an area thick with forests and dark meadows, sliced in two by a silver stream. She saw three sisters and three castles and a white horse galloping across open fields.

Ludmila lay down. She closed her eyes and let the vision come.

Asleep in the soil, a woman was roused by a twinge of pain. She wrapped her arms around herself, drew her knees up to her chin. Her pulse quickened. It resonated through the earth, carried rivulets of her blood through the land.

The woman stretched her slender body. She walked barefoot along the cliff. Her gown billowed over the edge. Her long hair danced upwards. She raised a hand to protect her falling eyes from the glare of the last rays of sun.

A shadow raced across the river and the land and the woman's face. She moved away from the edge as a golden cradle toppled from a rocky castle. She watched it fall into deep waters, sink into the sandy bed of the river. The waters swirled around the cradle, loosening the grainy sediment that held it in place, cleansing the mud that had sullied its radiance over centuries. It began to rise, glowing, incandescent as it neared the surface of the river, as if made of fire. The shadow lifted.

Ludmila stood and turned towards Prague.

She walked all the way back to the city. She went softly down Novy Svet to the House of the Golden Acorn. Inside, she was overwhelmed by a sense of everything Milena had felt and done during the three years they had been apart. She walked through the cottage, lightly touching furniture and objects. There was the cup

Milena drank from, there the bed she slept in, there the books she read. And there was the gift she had been given by the Puppet Master. Ludmila picked up the doll. She held it against her heart, stroked its long dark hair, wiped its wide dark eyes. She stepped back into the night and walked through the empty city towards Wenceslas Square, still clutching the doll.

It wasn't long before the House of the Ladies of the Snow came into view. She knocked on the door.

"Ludmila, come inside!" Tereza cried. She shepherded her sister inside. "You've been gone hours. Have you learned anything? Do you know where Milena might be?"

Ludmila pressed a finger to her lips. "Be calm, Tereza. How is Baba?"

"Katerina's with her. She hasn't said a word since we got home. But Katerina will see that she's back to her usual self in no time. Here she is now."

"Thank heavens you're home. We were so worried about you. Baba has finally fallen asleep. I think she's probably over the worst of it, but shock is an unpredictable condition. Come," said Katerina, putting an arm around Ludmila's waist. "I think I should examine you too, just to be sure."

Ludmila placed the Master's effigy of Milena on a table and began to speak.

"After you left the forest, Libuse came to me, as clear as if I had never sought to abandon her. I have seen what will come to pass. What must end, will soon end, what must be restored will soon be restored."

A loud knocking sounded at the door.

"I'll go," said Ludmila.

"Libuse!" cried Karel, his heart hammering in his chest. "You're safe. I was worried I was too late. Where's Milena?"

"Come inside. You're freezing."

"Thank you. Ever since I saw you in the cage, ever since the Master locked me up, all I've thought about is how I could make up for my foolishness, how I could help. I'm so sorry."

"There's time yet for you to help us. The Puppet Master still has my daughter."

"I'll do anything, anything at all."

"What's he doing here?" shouted Lukas, bolting down the hallway. "He works for the Master. Kick him out! I knew he couldn't be trusted but Milena wouldn't listen." He lunged at Karel.

"Don't worry, I know Karel," said Ludmila. "He's come to help us find Milena."

Lukas nodded, but still he seethed with anger. Why wouldn't anyone listen to him? How could they trust this stranger? For all they knew he could be in league with the Master.

Ludmila turned to Katerina and Tereza. "I must go to Milena. You stay with Baba and rest yourselves. Lukas, Karel, come with me."

The Hoof and the Horns and the Little White Bones

"Can't you find anything better for me to eat?" asked the Master, leaning over Milena's shoulder. "Is that the food of Kings? Is it?" He set himself down on a rock in the middle of the cave they had parked the wagon next to.

Milena stared hard at the pan of turnips she had been vainly trying to transform into soup. "You are *not* a king!" she exploded, kicking the pan into the fire. A misshapen turnip fell onto the feeble flames. "Stop saying that." She looked him up and down. "Who are you?" she demanded. "I mean, who are you *really*?"

"What kind of question is that? I am the Puppet Master, the Master of the Marionettes, descendent of he who should have been King of Bohemia. Bertoldo and I are as one, and you and your mother are the means by which I shall avenge the dishonour done to him. I intend to put your hitherto unleashed powers to very

good use, and there's no time like the present to begin your education. You must be ready to perform as soon as we have your mother back with us. You need to learn your script." He led Milena along the edge of the rocky ravine that plunged beneath the cave and up to the wagon.

Zdenka scowled as she watched Milena being escorted to warmth and shelter. She was beginning to wish they'd let the girl escape; the Master hadn't paid any attention to her or Zdenko since they'd arrived here.

"What do you need us to do?" Zdenka demanded, marching up to him and stamping her foot on the ground, eyes ablaze. "You said you had important work for us."

"Have patience, pretty puppet," he replied. "Jealousy is an ugly creature. Why don't you go for a wander and see if you can find me some fresh meat? Rabbit, or even a couple of squirrels will do. Whatever you find, I want them skinned and boiled in salt ready for my breakfast tomorrow. Perhaps we'll go on a little journey then. Perhaps we should leave Prague for a while. I need to revitalise my powers."

"I refuse to put up with this for this much longer," Zdenka huffed as soon as they were out of earshot. "If we're really so important to him, why are we the ones out in the cold running stupid errands while she lazes around in our Master's wagon? We're worth so much more than this. I'm not here to serve her. I won't do it." She flicked her plaits and pouted.

"He's bound to tire of her soon," said Zdenko. "Come on, let's have a look around the boneyard we passed on the way here."

The twins scuttled down the steep track that led to the Church of Saints Paul and Peter, and squeezed their way through the graveyard's iron gate. Moonlit and majestic, marble sculptures of angels garlanded with glistening cobwebs cast their shadows over the gravel path. Some of the graves were guarded by intimidating granite busts, others were adorned with carvings of flowers, cherubs and birds, according to the tastes of the deceased they honoured. Shiny red berries gleamed like rubies among the deep green shrubbery and trailing ivy filling the space between the headstones.

Zdenka took hold of her brother's arm. "Stop dragging me. Where are you rushing to?"

"You'll see," Zdenka smiled. "Look!"

"It can't be! I don't believe it," Zdenko cried. "I can see his horns!"

Diablovich appeared from behind a large mausoleum, whipping the air with his tail. He gnashed his teeth, pounded a clenched fist on the burial chamber.

"Actually, I'm not sure we should trust him. He looks…" Zdenka paused ". . . unpredictable."

"There's only one way to find out." Zdenko snapped his fingers. "Come to your Master, Diablovich. Come to me."

The marionette lowered his head, grasped hold of his golden horns and charged at the twins. They stood firm, even as Diablovich gained speed and hurtled ever closer to them. His over-sized foot slapped the path, propelling him faster and faster. Within a whisker of crashing into them, he ground to a sudden halt, kneeled and kissed Zdenko's silver-buckled shoes.

"He listened to you!" Zdenka gasped.

"Do you realise what this means?" Zdenko mused. "It means, dear sister, that we are still able to control the marionettes. It means the Master will need us more than ever. Perhaps Diablovich could help us revive the

other puppets. Perhaps they could bring the girl's mother to us."

"But if the Master doesn't show us the respect we deserve," Zdenka added, "I think we should take Diablovich and set up our own theatre. That would teach him to treat us like slaves."

She unfolded her arms, raised an eyebrow,crept around her brother with the lithe grace of a well-bred cat.

"Why don't we three sleep here tonight? I don't imagine the Master will allow us inside the wagon while his stupid princess is resting there."

"Good thinking. An exquisite act of cunning."

The twins settled in a mound of leaves behind the mausoleum. Diablovich stood over them, flicking his tail, scraping his hoof on the ground that concealed thousands and thousands of little white bones.

The Grasp of Good Hands

Ludmila drove the carriage through the city as fast as the horses would travel. They followed the course of the Vltava, raced down the lane past St. Martin's Rotunda, and stopped outside the Church of Saints Paul and Peter. "Follow me," she said, striding towards the cliffs of Vysehrad.

Lukas and Karel hadn't said a word to each other all the way there. They jostled to be first out of the carriage. But both stopped dead in their tracks when they saw the Master's wagon.

"Not so brave now, are you?" whispered Lukas.

"You're not exactly rushing to the rescue either," Karel replied. He paused. "This is silly. Don't we want the same thing? You might not trust me, but can we at least agree to be civil until Milena's safe?"

Reluctantly, Lukas nodded, suddenly aware of a plunging feeling in the pit of his stomach. It felt as if

he'd been dropped from a great height. Something had changed since he and Milena had met Karel. He sensed things would never be quite the same again.

"Mil-ena! Are you there?" he called.

The Master emerged from the wagon, constricting Milena's wrists with one hand, gripping Bertoldo's skull in the other. He moved closer to the edge of the cliff.

"Come for my pretty girl, have you?" he spat at Lukas. "She belongs to me now. She's mine to do with exactly as I want. And," he grinned, "unless you return her mother to me, I'll happily abandon her to the seas. She's as good as worthless to me if I don't have Libuse too. Where is she? What is it to be? Would you like to watch her drown?"

"You're ruined," shouted Karel. "Let go of her and take yourself away from here."

"Karel Kopecky? Now there's an unexpected treat! I didn't think I'd ever have the pleasure of seeing you again. I thought you'd be back in the filth of your father's farm by now. Now *where* is she?"

"There, look," said Zdenko, jumping from Diablovich's shoulders. "She's returned, like you said she would. But look, Master, we've brought your Devil back to life."

The twins stood either side of Diablovich, hands on hips, eyes shining like black marbles. "Did you miss us last night?" asked Zdenka.

Before the Master had chance to reply, the wagon door burst open and a group of marionettes tumbled down the steps.

"My darlings!" he cried. He focused his eyes on each in turn then clicked his fingers. "Capture them all!"

But the marionettes weren't listening to him. As though they had remembered how to walk, unaided they moved towards the Master, ferociously jerking their broken arms.

"This can't be true. No one else could control them. Zdenko, Zdenka, do something!"

"I told you he'd need us," Zdenko muttered to his sister. He snapped his fingers as hard and loud as he could. "Attack, Diablovich. Protect your Masters."

The Devil marionette thrust himself among the other puppets; fists flying, tail flicking. He snapped Hag Woman's head with a single twist of his wrist. The Jester somersaulted, kicked Diablovich to the ground as he flipped onto the floor. He leapt back and took a bow. Lady of Barley stuffed a fistful of feathers into the Devil's mouth while the rest of the group proceeded to grind him into little pieces. Soon, all that remained was a pile of wood, two golden horns and the fur from the tip of his tail. They turned as one and scrambled towards the Master.

"Come to me!" called Zdenko. "*We* are your leaders." But still the marionettes pushed forward, moving closer to the Master and Milena and the edge of the cliff.

"They'll kill him. I'm not going to die with him," whispered Zdenka. "Not after the way he neglected us. Let's go. Quickly." The twins linked arms and fled without as much as a backwards glance, their cloaks fluttering behind them like wings.

"Come back!" the Master ordered. "There are places for you at the side of my throne, remember."

Ludmila raised her arms. There was an eerie rumbling noise. The earth around the Master's boots began to crack. Lukas saw his grip on Milena slacken. He ran to her, dragging her to safety so fast it felt as if she were flying.

"Look out!" called Karel. "Step back."

The marionettes had forced the Puppet Master to the very edge of the cliff. He roared into the howling winds.

"My flame in this City of Snow and Ice is about to be extinguished, but I shall rise again in a City of Water."

It was the Story-teller who delivered the final fatal blow. He prodded the Master with his walking stick.

There was a crack of wood breaking and a fizz of amber sparks; the sound of the Master's body crashing against the cliff face as it fell into the Vltava. And as he plunged deeper and deeper through the water, towards the sandy bed, something began to rise. Something shiny, something golden.

"Can you see it?" asked Ludmila.

"Libuse's cradle!" Milena cried as the gleaming object emerged from the river.

"Come with me." Ludmila guided Milena down the rocky path. Everyone followed. Karel and Lukas heaved the bobbing cradle onto the shoreline. Milena laid both hands upon it and began to whisper.

"One day you shall emerge from the waters, purified by tears, and cleansed by the passing of time. And on that day, good hands will grasp you and lay within you a child who shall bring peace to this land."

Milena looked from Karel to Lukas to Ludmila. The winds subsided, the waters were calm, the earth ceased rumbling.

"One day we'll lay your firstborn in the cradle," Ludmila smiled.

Milena opened her eyes and looked to the north, to the heart of the city that nestled deep in the valley formed by seven hills. "Take me home to Prague."

Tuesday 18th January, 1898

TUESDAY 18TH JANUARY 1898

The Prague Daily

SPECIAL EDITION

CITY SAVED!

Milena Prochazkova and the city of Prague narrowly escaped tragedy yesterday when a Puppet Master's plot to seize control of Bohemia was foiled by the girl's mother, Ludmila Prochazkova, widow of renowned Prague puppeteer Petr Prochazka. Said to be a descendent of Libuse, the founder of our nation, Ludmila declined to comment on any hand her ancestress may or may not have had in yesterday's events.

It has emerged that the Master, who plunged to his death over the cliffs of Vysehrad, snatched dozens of Bohemian children during the past ten years, some of whom worked as labourers, while others were hypnotised and ghoulishly forced to be his living marionettes. Among them were Prague citizens Pavel Nezval and Ruzena Nezvalova, now reunited with their parents.

Ludmila Prochazkova thanked the Laskavy family, proprietors of The Place of Buttons & Boots on Nerudova Hill, for their support over the past weeks. Lukas Laskavy's role in the saving of the city and freeing Milena was 'absolutely vital.'

Karel Kopecky, a former marionette maker for the Puppet Master, was also praised. Kopecky has returned to his family in rural Eastern Bohemia, but plans to resume his career as a master marionette maker in the near future, perhaps even in the second incarnation of Petr Prochazka's theatre, *The House of Dream Delights*, which his widow and daughter have vowed to reopen as soon as they have secured the funds.

While the Master's reign of terror has ended, his closest allies, twins by the name of Zdenko and Zdenka, remain at large. The twins, who have never been seen apart from one another, are thought to have fled the country, but readers are requested to report any sightings of them to the authorities. **THEY ARE HIGHLY DANGEROUS.**

What Came to Pass

The city of Prague narrowly escaped tragedy yesterday when a Puppet Master's plot to seize control of Bohemia was foiled by Milena Prochazkova and her mother Ludmila, widow of renowned Prague puppeteer Petr Prochazka, said to be descendents of Libuse, the founder of our nation.

It has emerged that the Master, who plummeted to his death over the cliffs of Vysehrad, snatched dozens of Bohemian adults and children during the past ten years, some of whom worked as labourers, while others were hypnotised and ghoulishly transformed into living marionettes. Among them were Prague citizens Pavel Nezval and Ruzena Nezvalova, now reunited with their parents.

Ludmila Prochazkova and her daughter thanked the Laskavy family, proprietors of the Place of Buttons and Boots near Nerudova Hill, for their support. Lukas

Laskavy in particular played an "absolutely vital" role in the saving of the city and freeing his closest friend, Milena.

Karel Kopecky, a former marionette maker for the Puppet Master, was also praised. Kopecky has returned to his family in rural Eastern Bohemia, but plans to resume his career as a master marionette maker in the very near future in the second incarnation of Petr Prochazka's theatre, the House of Dream Delights, which his widow and daughter will reopen later this year.

Speaking from outside the theatre on Zelezna Street, Milena commented, "I can't wait to see marionettes return to Father's stage. It's going to be the *best* theatre in Prague."

While the Master's reign of terror has ended, his closest allies, twins by the name of Zdenko and Zdenka, remain at large. The twins, who have never been seen apart from one another, are thought to have fled the country, but readers are requested to report any sightings of them to the authorities. They are highly dangerous . . .

Author's Notes

Pronunciation Guide

The following Czech pronunciation guide might be handy when reading the notes and glossary.

a – like the "u" in "cup"
á – long "a" as in "far" or "large"
c – resembles the "ts" sound in "treats" or "hits"
č – the accent above this is called a hook or háček. The sound of "č" is like the "ch" sound in "cheese" or "Czech"
ch – resembles the "ch" of "loch"
ď – like "ty" in "duty"
é – lengthened, similar to the "a" in "care"
ě – insert a "y" sound before "e", e.g. němec (German) is pronounced "nyemets"
í – like the "ee" sound in "seed"
j – like the "y" sound in "yes"
ň – like "n" in "new"
ó – "o" lengthened as in "call"
r – rolled more than in English
ř – the most difficult sound in Czech, this is pronounced like an "r" with "ž", a little like the "s" sound in English "pleasure"
š – like English "sh" as in "ship"
ů – a long sound, like the "oo" in "hoop"
ý – like the "í" sound, the "ee" in "seed"
ž – similar to the "s" sound in "leisure"

A Note on Czech Surnames

Readers may have noticed that Milena and her father have slightly different surnames. This is because Czech surnames change according to whether a person is male or female. The general rule is that female surnames end in the suffix "-ova", so while Milena's Father's surname is Prochazka, hers is Prochazkova.

Inspiration and Legends

I'd always planned to write a book, but it wasn't until my first visit to Prague that I discovered the story and inspiration I'd been looking for. The writer Franz Kafka was right when he remarked in a letter to a friend that, "Prague doesn't let go. This little mother has sharp claws."

In *Puppet Master*, I have remained largely faithful to the legends of Libuše, prophetess and mythical mother of Prague as they were retold by Czech cultural revivalist Alois Jirásek (1851–1930) in his book *Staré pověsti české (Old Bohemian Legends)*, originally published in 1894. However, I did depart from tradition in my use of the story of Vlasta and Šarka – according to legend, the women were eventually defeated – and the figure of Brother Bertoldo is entirely fictitious.

Czech Marionette Tradition

As anyone who has visited Prague will know, marionettes (*loutka* in Czech) enjoy a strong presence in the city. The tradition first arrived in Bohemia in the sixteenth century when troupes from Italy and Austria, Holland and Germany converged in the heart of Europe. The first recorded puppet show in Prague dates from 1563 and in the centuries that followed several dynasties of marionette-making families were established, the most famous of which was that founded by Jan Kopecký whose name is first mentioned in 1779. He passed on his skills to his son, Matěj, widely believed to be the greatest of all Czech puppeteers.

During the mid- to late-nineteenth century, the influence of marionette theatre was wide, often crossed into other forms of art, and was enjoyed by all ages. In the early days adaptations of classic stories like *Faust* were common, while from the beginning of the twentieth century performances of fairytales became increasingly popular.

Glossary

Absinthe

Highly intoxicating translucent green spirit distilled from wormwood.

The Astronomical Clock

Czech – *orloj*. The technical and aesthetic wonder visitors still gather around today was added to the tower of the Old Town Hall *(Staroměstská radnice)* on Old Town Square *(Staroměstské náměstí)* by Master Hanuš in 1490.

Babovka

Czech – *bábovka*. A traditional Czech coffee cake baked in a deep, circular pan with a hole in the middle. Bábovka is often flavoured with either vanilla or chocolate.

Bohemia

A region in the north west of the present-day Czech Republic. The other main areas are Moravia in the east and Slovakia (now the Slovak Republic) in the south.

Burdock

A plant traditionally believed to have healing and protection properties.

Certovka

Czech – *čertovka,* meaning Little Devil. A small fork of the Vltava that divides Kampa Island from the Lesser Quarter.

Devil's Apple

Also known as *Thornapple, Datura, Stinkweed* and *Devil's Trumpet*. A poisonous plant that has been used in shamanic rites for centuries, it is said to ward off evil spirits, protect the home and cure insomnia.

Divoka Sarka

Czech – *Divoka Šarka*, meaning Wild Sarka. A character from Bohemian mythology and the name of a rugged park and area of woodland located to the north-west of present day Prague.

Emperor Rudolf II

The eccentric Hapsburg ruler who moved his court from Vienna to Prague in 1583. Under his rule Prague became not only the heart of the Hapsburg Empire but also a centre of artistic, scientific and alchemical exploration.

Golden Lane

Czech – *zlatá ulička*. Located within the grounds of Prague Castle, Golden Lane comprises a row of tiny, picturesque, brightly painted cottages. Some say the name derives from the days when Emperor Rudolf's alchemists lived here, but more likely the street took its name from the city's goldsmiths who worked here in the seventeenth century. In 1917 author Franz Kafka lived at no. 22 in his sister's cottage.

Henbane

Also known as *Devil's Eye, Hogsbean* and *Black Nightshade*, this highly poisonous plant was traditionally used to induce love. When burned outdoors it is said to bring the rain.

Horehound

This plant is traditionally used in protection charms. Drinking an infusion of horehound is said to clear the mind and strengthen mental prowess.

Hradcany

Czech *hrad* – castle. *Hradčany* is the Czech name for Prague's Castle District which was founded in the early fourteenth century. It was mainly a Quarter for the nobility, with the exception of *Nový Svět* which was long home to the district's poorest residents. Notable landmarks include Prague Castle itself *(Pražský hrad)*, the Strahov Monastery *(Strahovské nádvoři)* and the Loreta Square *(Loretánské náměstí)*

Hypnosis

A sleep-like condition that renders people highly susceptible to the suggestion of the hypnotist.

Josefev

The medieval Jewish Quarter of Prague, located on the right bank of the Vltava. Notable landmarks include the oldest synagogue in Europe, Old-New Synagogue *(Staronová synagoga)* and the Old Jewish Cemetery *(Starý židovský hřbitov)*.

Karlovy Vary

An old spa town in Western Bohemia.

Karluv Bridge

Czech – *Karlův Most* meaning Charles Bridge. Linking the Old Town and the Lesser Quarter, the first stone bridge on this site was built in 1357 after its predecessor, Judith Bridge, collapsed in a flood in 1342. The statues lining the bridge were added in the seventeenth century. Today replicas of the originals stand in their place.

Krkonose

Czech – *Krkonoše* meaning Giant Mountains. A mountain range in East Bohemia that borders with Poland's Silesia region.

Limet

Bitter herb liqueur with lemons and a touch of cinnamon.

Linden trees

Czech – *lípa*. Also known as lime trees, these are the national tree of the Czech Republic and are highly revered in Germanic mythology. Linden tree timber is soft and easily worked and is often used to make marionettes.

Mala Strana

Czech – *Malá Strana* meaning Lesser Quarter. Located on the left bank of the Vltava and founded in 1287. Notable landmarks include the Lesser Quarter Square *(Malostranské náměstí)*, the Church of Saint Nicholas, the Maltese Square *(Maltézské náměstí)* and Petrin Hill *(Petřínské sady*, see below).

Nove Mesto

Czech – *Nové Město* meaning New Town. Located to the south of the Old Town, this district was founded in 1348 when Charles IV *(Czech-Karel)*, King of the Golden Age of Bohemia, decreed that Prague needed a new, modern town. Principle landmarks include Wenceslas Square *(Václavské náměstí)* with its statue of St. Wenceslas *(Czech- sv. Václav)* and the National Museum.

Novy Svet

Czech – *Nový svět* meaning new world. A street in the Castle District that has been home to a number of famous residents, including Tycho Brahe, astrologer to Emperor Rudolph II, and the Czech violin virtuoso Ondříček.

Petrin Hill

Czech – *Petřínské sady*. The most peaceful of Prague's seven hills and the largest green area in the city. Notable landmarks include the Hunger Wall *(Hladova zed')* commissioned by Charles IV in 1362 to occupy Prague's poor, the Mirror Maze *(Zrcadlové bludiště)*, Petřín Tower *(Rozhledna)*, the Štefánik Observatory *(Hvězdárna),* and the funicular railway.

Prague

Czech – *Praha*. Capital of the region of Bohemia and the Czech Republic.

Stare Mesto

Czech – *Staré Město* meaning Old Town. The medieval heart of Prague whose notable landmarks include Powder Gate *(Prašná brána)*, the Old Town Square *(Staroměstské náměstí)* and the Astronomical Clock *(orloj)*.

St. Vitus's Cathedral

Czech – *Katedrála sv.Víta*. Located in the third courtyard of Prague Castle, the Gothic steeples of St. Vitus's Cathedral dominate the city's skyline and stands where Svaṭovit, the Slavic god of fertility, was worshipped in Pagan times.

Slivovice

A smooth plum brandy.

Smetana, Bedřich

(1824-1884) Esteemed Czech composer whose work often explored Czech myths and themes e.g. My Homeland *(Má Vlast)*, Libuše and The Bartered Bride *(Prodaná nevěsta)*.

Sticklewort

Also known as Agrimony and Church Steeples, this plant was used to detect the presence of witches and is said to make one sleep like the dead when placed beneath the head.

Virginia dogwood

Also known as Budwood, Dogtree and Green Osier, this plant is said to possess wish-granting properties and to protect those who wear an amulet containing its leaves.

Vltava

The Czech Republic's longest river. It cuts through the centre of Prague, runs north into the Elbe and streams into the North Sea in Hamburg.

Vysehrad

Czech – *Vyšehrad* meaning castle *(hrad)* on a high place. A district on the south west banks of the Vltava, mythological home of Libuše and the Přemyslid dynasty. Notable landmarks include Vyšehrad Cemetery, the Church of Saints Paul and Peter *(Pavel and Petr)* and Josef Václav Myslbek's sculptures of Libuše, Přemsyl, Šarka and Ctirad.

A note about the illustrations

To create the illustrations and images for *Puppet Master*, Mutt Ink used various means to visualise the author's words. Our many resources for reference included objects and textures, archival photos, original documents from the seventeenth and eighteenth centuries (including paper and handwritten script from antique marriage certificates and diaries), junk shop finds, vintage posters, books, and even autumnal garden leaves, as well as a large amount of personal reference supplied by the author.

We conceived the illustrations by hand and composed each piece digitally using Adobe Photoshop and Illustrator. Layer upon layer of artwork and subtle colour gives each piece its own unique richness, at the same time maintaining the mystery and drama of the content.

Joanne was born in Pembrokeshire, Wales, and read Social and Political Sciences with Archaeology and Anthropology at St John's College, Cambridge.

Now living in north London, by day Joanne works in children's publishing, by night she writes and plays bass guitar and accordion.

Puppet Master is her first novel.